The Truth about Alicia
and Other Stories

Camino del Sol
A Latina and Latino Literary Series

The Truth about Alicia and Other Stories

Ana Consuelo Matiella

The University of Arizona Press
Tucson

The University of Arizona Press
© 2002 Ana Consuelo Matiella
First Printing

This book is printed on acid-free, archival-quality paper.
Manufactured in the United States of America

07 06 05 04 03 02   6 5 4 3 2 1

Library of Congress Cataloging-in-Publication Data

Matiella, Ana Consuelo.
    The truth about Alicia and other stories / Ana Consuelo Matiella.
        p. cm. — (Camino del sol)
    ISBN 0-8165-2161-1 —
    ISBN 0-8165-2163-8 (pbk.)
    1. Mexican American families — Fiction. 2. Mexican American
    women — Fiction. 3. Mexican Americans — Fiction. I. Title II. Series.
    PS3613.A83 T7 2002
    813'.54 — dc21   2001003544

British Library Cataloguing-in-Publication Data
A catalogue record for this book is available from the British Library.

"Angels" was previously published in *Walking the Twilight*, by Northland
Publishing.

Publication of this book is made possible in part by the proceeds of a
permanent endowment created with the assistance of a Challenge Grant
from the National Endowment for the Humanities, a federal agency.

To Papá Pepe, who long ago thanked God because there were no stupid people in our family. To Tío Romeo and Tía Paqui for loving me by telling me stories. To Ron for helping me find Crow, Miriam for being the best midwife, las parteras of Franklin Avenue for assisting in labor, and to my Sari-Sari for blessing me with the essence of daughter love.

Contents

*The Truth about Alicia
and Other Stories*

Nana's Trilogy

Prologue

Before I pitched the handful of soft desert earth on the red roses
and black coffin, I remembered that Nana's skin was brown. Her
eyes were wild and gray and spoke silently of untellable stories.
Her hands were a working woman's hands that washed clothes on
washboards, that tied nooses around plump chickens' necks and
dunked them in boiling water before dinner without hesitation.
The dry yellow spot on her forefinger flicked the ashes of
countless hand-rolled cigarettes.

I spent eternal hot afternoons sometimes following her,
sometimes hiding silently from her, in between what was there
and what was not.

I   La Pajarera

La pajarera was the woman who sold birds, carrying her birdcages
stacked on her shoulders, very high.

She passed by Nana's once a week with her birds and herbs. I could tell that my grandmother was afraid of her. Whenever Nana saw her coming up the front porch steps, she would quickly close the venetian blinds so la pajarera couldn't peek in. She called her vieja bruja—old witch.

La pajarera sold green and yellow parrots and canaries and passed by when it was screechy hot. Her skin was grayish green, like a lizard's. When she squinted and smiled, her face creased into a thousand rivers.

One day when she stopped by, I was playing jacks on the porch by the lilac bush. "Y esta muchachita tan bonita, ¿quién es?" she asked in her singsong tone. "And who is this little girl, so pretty?"

I looked up and saw her birds, her face sandwiched between the cages. She was looking at the wall. She acted like she was asking someone else, not me.

"I'm going to give her a blessing. No one will cast a spell on her. No one can give her the evil eye," she said to the mosaic of the holy family on the wall. "Pa' que no me la vayan a hechizar."

She licked her thumb, which came at me still smelling of saliva. She made the sign of the cross on my forehead. Her thumb was coarse, like a cat's tongue.

I sat there looking up at her wrinkled face. Still feeling the sticky cross on my forehead, I screamed.

My grandmother shot through the screen door with the force of a powerful push from behind. With her large purple broom and a mouth full of words we weren't allowed to repeat, she ran la pajarera off the porch.

The old bird woman quickly gathered her cages and went on her way, muttering to herself.

With too much fear in her eyes, Nana flew inside for the

holy water. She doused and sprinkled and prayed the thirty-three creeds. After that, she made us both a good strong glass of sugared water for the fright. She gulped hers down, her eyes almost popping out of their sockets.

I went back to the porch, playing jacks by the lilac bush. I smelled of saliva and holy water.

From then on, every unfortunate thing that happened to me was blamed on the curse of la pajarera—amoebas, chickenpox, the time I punctured my knee with a nail at Doña Pelona's, every time I talked back to my mother, and when I refused to go back to catechism.

II Blue Dog

When the old gringo, Mr. Zisk, gave us the weimaraner, we were excited. My father said weimaraners were a rare breed and this one was worth a lot of money.

His eyes and his coat were blue. His tongue was pink, and he looked like no other dog. We named him Blue.

We took the pup across the border to my grandmother's house, and all the cousins and the swarm of neighborhood children came out to look at him.

Romero, the orphan boy who lived at Doña Chana's house, said the dog was endiablado, full of the devil. My brother, Francisco, already attached to Blue, told him, "Chinga tu madre, if you can find her."

Romero was silenced. We all knew he had been given to Doña Chana to work on the yard, feed the chickens, run errands, and be of good use. He had no mother.

"Come on, Manita," my brother said to me. "Let's get out of here." And he held Blue close to him, like a baby.

We went back to Nana's house, and I went inside to have bread and café con leche. Francisco tied Blue to a fence post by the rabbit pen behind the kitchen. Through the old pink screen of the kitchen window, I could see Francisco talking to Blue. The dog was nodding as if they were having a conversation.

My grandmother looked through the screen too, but she seemed worried. "Go tell your brother to come in for a cup of café con leche and sweet bread."

I motioned with my chin and said, "Not yet, he's talking to the blue dog."

She moved closer to the window and peered out, trying to listen. "Heaven help us if that dog talks back. Francisco will end up like Julio, down the street. He talked to his pigeons. When the pigeons answered him, he dropped dead, poor thing."

My heart was beating in my throat. I told Nana what Doña Chana's boy said—that Blue had the devil inside him. Her ashen mouth muttered, "Ave Maria Purísima."

That afternoon my father came to pick us up. We all went to our grandfather's farm, about thirty-five miles south into Mexico. The summer afternoon had promised rain, and the pastures between Nogales and Magdalena were bright green. The puffy clouds inhaled deeply and filled their cheeks, ready for the storm. Blue was in a cardboard box in the back of our stationwagon.

When we got to the farm, Don Jacinto, the mayordomo, came out to greet us. He and the adults shook hands. When he saw the puppy, he said, "¡Qué perro tan raro!" Don Jacinto and Nana exchanged knowing glances about Blue's strangeness.

We let Blue out of the box, and then we all chased piglets, and the chickens jumped on the roofs, trying to get away. "Stay away from the well," my father warned. "Stay away from the well."

The well was behind the house. We were never supposed to go near a well, any well. We'd heard many stories about children falling in wells and drowning. Once two brothers drowned, one trying to save the other.

The day got still as the clouds got darker. Animals scattered in all directions, seeking shelter. All the children went inside except Francisco and me. "Where's Blue?" my brother asked. We called his name and looked all over, but we couldn't find him. He wasn't by the chicken coop and he wasn't roaming around the orange grove. He was nowhere.

"Blue! Blue!" my brother called, his voice thick with fear.

I told him not to go near the well, that Dad would be angry, that he would get it with the belt, but he didn't listen. "Blue's in there," he said, straddling the well's short adobe wall, crystalline tears running down his red cheeks. When I screamed for help, Dad came running out of the back of the house. His swift yank landed Francisco safely outside the well. My brother's body fell face down upon the soft red earth. He heaved back and forth as he wept. My father let me look in. Blue was floating, stiff and lifeless, on the dark, shiny surface.

I looked into Nana's eyes, and when she looked away, I knew what she had done.

III Crow

I fought an afternoon sleep to watch Crow dance on a wire. He had something to show me in his gold beak. He bobbed his head, signaling he wanted to talk.

"You see, little one, in this picture your grandmother has no hair. See how she is dressed like a boy? That was the only way she could go outside. The Villistas had gone crazy-crazy by then.

Anyone, rich or poor, young, old, Indian, mestizo or Creole, could be next.

"War does that to people. It makes them crazy and erases the lines between one thing and another. It's like when I fly upside down. I lose the sky.

"Your Nana was raised in Ures, Sonora, during the Mexican Revolution. The Villistas raided the villages and took what they wanted, sacks of flour and young girls.

"No one knew how to protect her from the raids. So Pa Joaquín decided, 'Shave her head and dress her in Raul's clothes. We need all the help we can get.' Mama Kina was worried. 'The girl is fifteen, Joaquín. She should be going to dances, dressed in long dresses,' she said. But Pa Joaquín was a practical man.

"Head shaved, dressed in her brother's clothes, with a dark gray felt hat over her ears, she could feed the chickens and the rabbits and milk the goats.

"Do you know what the Villistas did to the old Frenchman, Don Fabian? They burned his restaurant and bodega down to ashes; no more than four tables fit into his little place. They didn't even drink the wine from his beloved wine cellar. They broke the bottles and the old wooden barrels and set the whole place on fire. Don Fabian knelt at the doorway and wept while the town looked on, waiting to see who'd be next.

"And what about old Donadieu? He played dead on the train they raided, but one of the soldiers liked his ruby ring so much he chopped Donadieu's finger right off with a machete. Just like that. Donadieu didn't bat an eyelash. He figured better to give up his finger now and join Fabian later for a good game of dominoes.

"Shaved head, dressed like a boy, your Nana heard the sound of the horses trotting. She heard the sound of a cruel man's laughter. She ran and the fear made her fly, and her flight turned her upside down.

"For a time after Pa Joaquín found her, she didn't know if the sky was brown or if the mud was blue and she didn't understand the blue puddles on the soft earth after the rain.

"It was a time when lines were erased and people didn't know if they were here or there. Sometimes your Nana knew which way was up and which way was down. Sometimes she laughed, knowing the blue in the puddle was the reflection of the sky. And sometimes she cried desperately, digging in the muddy hole to pull the blue out.

"That is why she drowned your dog. That is why she knew la pajarera would put a hex on you. And that is why I come and tell you these things."

When Crow stopped talking, my ears were ringing loud and I couldn't tell if I was asleep or awake. I stumbled through a dark place to find a question. I asked, "Crow, the cicadas buzz louder than usual today. Do you know why?"

He murmured, "Sleep, little one. The day is forbiddingly hot and you already know much more than your share."

Crow's wings cut a black silhouette out of the blue sky.

Angels

You can feel their presence sometimes — a brush of a soft wing, a light kiss on the eyelids while you sleep — but to actually see an angel is not good for your longevity.

My grandfather encountered several angels and lived to tell about them, but that's why he died young. Nana said that he was on his way to becoming an angel himself and so had an ease of communication with celestial beings.

Although I love my angels and sometimes leave little trinkets for them to play with or open books for them to read at night, I would much rather not come across them by sight, if you know what I mean.

It's the same with animals. Nana told me there was once a boy who lived in our old barrio. His name was Julio and he talked to his pigeons and they talked back and he died. Nana said he died because it's all right for you to talk to animals, but if they respond, it's too much for a human being.

Me, I don't mind talking to animals, especially dogs. They

are the most dear to me, although I am somewhat infatuated with crows. But to tell you the truth, I am afraid of an audible response. So when I ask an animal a question, I always stop and say, "Please don't answer that."

I have always feared crossing over to the world where animals talk back and angels make special appearances because I lack the courage to deal with them. But there are things that I know and stories I've heard that lead me to believe in angels and the conversational capabilities of certain animals.

Take what happened to Heidi, for example. Heidi died in Magdalena, Sonora, in a house facing the acequia that irrigated the dusty corn crops. She was eight years old. I can still remember her face in the black-and-white photograph my mother brought back from the funeral I wasn't allowed to go to.

Heidi and I didn't meet until after she died, when she smiled at me from her first communion photograph. She was kneeling down and looking up at the Sacred Heart of Jesus, a pearl rosary hanging from her two small hands.

"She looks like an angel," I told Nana, lightly touching the smooth surface of the photograph. "She was an angel," my grandmother explained. "She was too good, and God called her to help out someplace else. That's what happens. God takes the good ones and leaves the rotten ones for us to contend with."

I wondered how she died. Heidi would never have gone out to the slippery banks of the flooded irrigation ditch by herself, I reasoned. She sat by the old Philco every Saturday afternoon to listen to the *Lone Ranger*. Heidi embroidered little dish towels for her aunt and helped her mother in the kitchen. She never said "I don't want to" to her mother, or "That's not true."

Nana said she was so good she had a star on her forehead.

But one day, one of the only times she disobeyed her mother, she got up from the obligatory siesta in the height of a hot afternoon. She went to the backyard and peered inside the family well. In the reflection of the water below, she saw a pair of angel wings behind her, opalescent pink and white. Startled, she ran inside the house, where she was immediately punished and given orange blossom tea to calm her nerves.

She died and no one ever told me how. She died and I didn't get a chance to meet her until after the funeral, when I held a black-and-white photograph of her in my hands. It was midday on a boring summer afternoon in Magdalena. I was supposed to be sleeping, and only the lizards were out, hissing back at the noon-day sun.

I often thought about Heidi and wondered how and why she died. I asked my grandmother, "Did she die because a child is not supposed to see the angels? Was it like Julio talking to his pigeons and the pigeons talking back?"

I repeatedly asked Nana about Heidi, but Nana didn't want to talk. My grandfather had also just died, and I think it was too soon for her to talk about angels.

On another occasion, feeling the emptiness my grandfather's death created in the house, I asked Nana, "Why did Tata have to die?"

She didn't look up. She said, "He died because he talked to the angels and the angels talked back. There are people who meet angels face to face every day and don't know it. But your Tata was different. He knew an angel when he saw one. He was too good for this world and he knew too much."

Then she told me about the time they were traveling to Ures, Sonora, for the Feast of the Epiphany.

When Mama and my Aunt Paqui were still little girls, about ten and thirteen years old, the family set out for Ures to see their maternal grandmother, Mama Kina. It was January 5, the eve of the Feast of the Epiphany.

Although the road from Nogales to Ures was open, it hadn't been paved. When it rained, summer or winter, the soft desert earth turned into silt and slush. Cars would get stuck and have to be retrieved by a team of mules.

During the holiday season it was Tata's custom to collect old clothes, blankets, and used toys for some of the poor children who lived on the family ranch. On this late evening the family packed Tata's old Model T truck full of stuff and took off for Ures on their annual Christmas journey.

It was a cold and rainy night, and they were sloshing down the deserted road, loudly singing Mexican rancheras to pass the time. The children had hopes of waking up at the ranch to find little trinkets and candy left to them by the Three Kings. Nana and Tata were looking forward to a midnight dinner of Mama Kina's tamales.

Out of nowhere, a man swinging a lantern walked across the road and stopped right in front of the truck. Tata slammed on his brakes, and the overloaded truck fishtailed on the slippery road.

When the truck finally came to a stop, Tata was furious. The man with the lantern was standing by a mesquite tree directly across the road from where Tata had had to swerve to miss him. How was it possible that the man with the lantern had gotten across the road to the mesquite tree?

The stranger, quiet and reserved, leaned against the tree waiting for Tata to get out of the truck. Nana was convinced he was Satan. Her flesh was crawling with goose pimples, and the children were crying. Tata ordered them to stay in the truck and lock the doors. Nana began to pray her rosary, and all the children echoed their reply.

In those days Tata always carried a pistol. He tapped his pistol to see if it was still there, then got out of the truck. He walked over to the man with the lantern. In anger Tata confronted the man, demanding, "Are you a madman or what?"

The man answered, "Buenas noches, Pancho. Forgive that I startled you and your family, but . . ."

Tata interrupted. "How do you know my name?"

The man shrugged and smiled, saying, "I know many things that would surprise you, Pancho, but never mind. The left rear wheel of that old truck of yours is loose, and it is dangerous on such a rainy night . . ."

Stunned and scared, Tata hesitantly responded, "The wheels of the truck are fine, my friend. You are the one who has a loose wheel in that head of yours."

The man with the lantern was silent and merely pointed to the wheel. At the moment he pointed, the wheel fell right off the axle and the truck plunked down and hit the ground lopsided.

My grandfather was shocked and turned immediately to the stranger — to thank him for his good deed, to ask him how he knew, to offer him one of his homemade chorizos and a shot of tequila. But when he looked up, the stranger was gone.

Tata felt the hairs on his back stand up; he broke into a cold sweat. Knees weak, he sat on a large rock by the mesquite tree, trying to keep his heart from racing and his hands from shaking. He sat there listening to the sounds of the light winter drizzle for a few moments before he attended to the fallen wheel.

After the family recuperated from the ordeal, they started on their way to Ures again. Nana said that Tata got back in the driver's seat and took a shot of tequila, made the sign of the cross, and closed his eyes. When he opened his eyes he said, "Concha, that was not a mortal man."

Silence set in and they drove for a few miles. Tata, breathing a sigh of relief, looked out into the dark and rainy desert. He wasn't surprised at what he saw. He turned to Nana and the children and said, "Look, up there!"

Up on top of a distant hill, in the deep blue, they saw a lantern waving back and forth in the dark.

Feliz Navidad

My grandfather died when I was two, but he came to me one Christmas Eve when I was five years old and I was sick with the croup. From where I lay, I could hear the laughter coming from the kitchen where my parents, aunts and uncles, and grandmother sat around gossiping, laughing, and teasing one another.

The women made tamales while the men ate and drank hot tequila calientitos with cinnamon and cloves. The steam of the tamales fogged the windows of the small adobe house. I could see through part of the glass where the cooled-off steam came streaking down. The small bedroom where I lay was connected to the kitchen by the bathroom. The bedroom was painted a glossy lime green. Outside, the night was dark and royal blue.

I was not alone. St. Francis of Assisi also lay in the green room. St. Martin, St. Anthony, and Our Lady of Guadalupe had their nichos there, and nailed to the wall was the crucifix that had been part of my grandfather's burial service. The mortician gave it to my grandmother right before the first fistful of dirt was thrown on Tata's casket. We called this room "el cuarto de los santos."

St. Francis was on his deathbed. His was the only other bed there besides mine. He lay on a long wooden table with a white shroud trimmed with lace edges draped over his emaciated body. Many times, on my way to the bathroom, I had stopped to pay my reluctant respects. I had seen the unforgettable stigmata on his crossed hands and feet, had touched his slender face and looked into his glassy eyes.

The only other San Francisco I had seen like this one was much bigger and resided in the church in Magdalena, Sonora, where every October thousands of faithful worshippers came from miles around to lift his heavy head. The lifting of St. Francis's head signified the weighing of your sins. If you could lift his head easily and plant a kiss on his forehead, it meant that you didn't have so many sins. If his head was hard to lift, it meant you were burdened by your sins and needed to repent.

But on this day in the saint's green room, the santos danced with the flames of the votive candles and I had a fever.

"It's the fever," my aunts and uncles reassured my grand-mother. They tried to convince her that I could not have seen my grandfather. My grandfather was dead.

I had been sitting up watching St. Anthony's shadow dance on the wall when my grandfather came and sat next to me on the bed. His belly was still as round as I remembered, and he was still wearing the khaki uniform he wore in all the family photos.

"Maria Antonieta," he said clearly.

"Tata, what are you doing here?" I asked. My hands and feet suddenly felt cold, and I could hear my teeth chattering. I was afraid.

"I came to see my granddaughter."

"But you're dead, Tata," I said.

He laughed so loud I was sure they could hear him in the kitchen. His laughter made me feel at ease. Out of nowhere he produced a red mesh Christmas stocking, like the kind they had at Woolworth's. It was full of tiny toys and good things to eat: a little black clay doll with real fine black hair, a wooden top, a yo-yo, hard Christmas candies, an orange, and walnuts.

He emptied the contents of the stocking on my lap and sat on the edge of the creaky brass bed, watching me play. I was delighted with the surprise. But when I looked up to show him the black dolly, he was gone.

"Tata! Tata!" I cried. "¿Dónde estás?"

My mother rushed in. "What's the matter, mija?" She looked at my lap with the empty red mesh stocking and the toys scattered on the bed.

"I told you not to look in the bag. Now you've ruined the surprise!" She sounded irritated.

"Where's Tata?" I asked.

"Your Tata is in heaven, mijita, with the angels!"

"No, Mami," I said, "he was just here. He gave me this." I held up the empty stocking as proof.

"Yeah, yeah, and I'm Tarzan's mother," she said in a skeptical tone.

"Tata!" I shrieked.

That's when my Aunt Paqui and the rest of my aunts and uncles came in. My grandmother nervously checked the mustard patch on my chest and touched my forehead. "She doesn't feel very hot."

"Where's Tata?" I asked again.

"Ave Maria Purísima," Nana said, making the sign of the cross. "What are you saying, child?"

"Mi Tata ..." I sobbed. "Mi Tata!"

She made a beeline for the holy water.

My mother sat next to me and tried to calm me down. Her round eyes got bigger, and she took both my hands in hers. "You have a fever, mija. Calm down and go to sleep. Tonight, after you go to sleep, Santa Claus will come and bring you that doll you wanted with the blue dress. Let me give you the blessing."

She made the sign of the cross, starting at my forehead. "In the name of the Father and of the Son and of the Holy Spirit."

By the time she got to my left shoulder, I was dozing off. The blessing always made me sleepy.

I could hear them murmuring to each other as they walked out of the green room.

My father, who subscribed to a much simpler form of Catholicism, said, "What do you expect, Emma? That pinche room looks like the San Ramón Chapel."

My Tía Paqui said, "Poor little thing. It must be a high fever for her to be so delirious like that."

My Uncle Romeo said, "Quite an imagination on that one."

Nana was worried. "Ay, Holy Jesus, what a fright! Do you think Pancho would really come to her like that?"

Uncle Beto said, "Ay, amà. Don't get yourself all worked up. She's just a kid with a fever!"

Nana was still worried. "I don't know, mijo. You know what they say ... crazy people and children always tell the truth."

And from my bed in el cuarto de los santos I said, "Good night, Tata. Feliz Navidad."

Sana, Sana, Colita de Rana

The Hail Mary throbbed in waves. The rise and fall of the women's voices created a hypnotizing rhythm. It mattered little what they were saying. What mattered was the power of their voices and the sadness in their faces, seething. Dark women in black lace mantillas mourning my mother, La India Bonita.

We come from a place where if you are fat, they call you "gordo"; if you are short, they call you "chapo"; if you are ugly, they call you "feo". I am the son of a Yaqui Indian woman. They called her India, La India Bonita.

The break in the voices brought me back to the present. I had been remembering the house on Morita Street....

We found the big house on Morita when I was about eight years old. Uncle Teo drove us right up to the front yard in his black 1949 Packard. It was a dusty Nogales, Sonora, day. The sun was so bright my eyes ached after we walked under the cool shade of the long green portal. Two large leather rocking chairs, one on each side of the screen door, welcomed us. Adorning the front of the wide screen door was a wrought-iron peacock painted forest green. The door was heavy to open and slammed promptly behind us with the hostile vengeance meant for flies.

The long hallway, dark and cool, was tiled in a simulated green marble.

Uncle Teo was excited. "What did I tell you, India?"

"It's too big for Cali and me, Teo—you know that. What do I want with a four-bedroom house?"

"It's a good deal, hermana … wait till you see the little orchard in the back. The old gachupín even built a chicken coop. And there's room for that worthless Gaetan of yours. Come on, I'll show you."

Gaetan was our blue tick hound. He came to us one dreary night, hungry and depressed, howling at our doorstep. His blood-shot eyes reminded my mother of Great Uncle Queno, so we took him in. The first thing Mama and I did was bathe him and dip him in insecticide because he was so full of ticks and fleas. Later Mama, an avid encyclopedia reader, looked him up under "Dogs." From the pictures, he looked most like a blue tick hound, so from that day on that is what he was.

"A blue tick hound," Mama said. "Qué bien. A very distinguished-looking dog. Let's see, what should we name him, Cali? Since he looks like an old French gentleman, let's call him Gaetan. Yes, that's it, Gaetan. It's very French."

In Nogales anything French was considered distinguished. Gaetan, in addition to being distinguished, had a remarkable sense of justice and howled miserably when we tied him up. So we were looking for a place with a yard.

"You're crazy, Teo. A saleslady from Bracker's can't afford a house like this," she said with one of her flashiest smiles.

At the time we rented the house on Morita Street, it was

only Mama, me, and Gaetan. Uncle Teo had dinner with us once or twice a week. After dinner Mama and Teo had coffee and we all played Chinese checkers out on the portal. Mama always won.

The adobe house was comfortable and cool, and the old Spaniard who owned it had a strong preference for the color forest green. All the ledges, windowsills, and doors were painted in that color.

Mama took the front bedroom by the portal with the flower garden on the southwest side. The old Spaniard, who was known as El Gachupín, had taken good care of the house. And to his credit, despite the Sonoran Desert sun, the garden was beautiful, mostly rose bushes and dahlias in purple, bright orange, and red.

I took the long bedroom on the other side of the bathroom I shared with Mama. It had new linoleum with a giant pink and blue flower print. Two long windows overlooked the back end of the garden and a large empty lot that served as the neighborhood playground. The other two bedrooms were empty for quite some time. Eventually one of the bedrooms doubled as Mama's sewing room and Olga's bedroom, and the room at the end of the hall, with its own entrance, was reserved for Uncle Teo for when he came to Nogales from his ranch in Imuris.

When Teo was home, Mama always cooked a full breakfast. In the mornings the house smelled of fresh roasted coffee, chorizo con huevo, Teo's orange blossom cologne, and stale beer.

I wanted to be tall and dark and wear pointed cowboy boots, like Teo. I envied his thick mustache. It was better than Emiliano Zapata's. He defined manhood for me in my early years. And although I managed to come to my own definition of manhood, I always referred to Teo's when I was lost.

Olga didn't come to us until later.

She came to us much as Gaetan did, hungry and depressed. I was nine years old when she knocked on the iron peacock, which by then had multicolored feathers. Mama had gotten tired of forest green.

It was Saturday, and I had converted the green hallway into a raceway for my tin can trucks. Olga peered in through the dark screen door. I could see her but she couldn't see me. She called out in a martyr's voice, full of melancholy and pain, "Buenas ta-a-ardes!"

I replied, "Good afternoon," and walked up to the dark screen door. When I saw that her feet were full of dust and her huaraches were old, I said, "What do you want?"

"Is your mama home? I have some hand-crocheted tablecloths to sell."

"She's in the garden. Wait here. I'll get her." I ran to the back door and called, "Mama, there's a vieja out front. Wants to see you."

An angry look told me I should have said "señora" instead of "old woman."

Olga waited patiently on the other side of the iron peacock for my mother to come. She carefully took a white tablecloth out of an old pillowcase. The tablecloth was white, with edges of stiff lace.

"¿Cuánto?" Mama asked, feeling the tablecloth between her thumb and her forefinger.

"Just a hundred pesos, señora," Olga said in her saddest singsong voice. "I just got here from Tepic and I'm looking for work. I am a good worker, señora. Do you want me to come in and make you some fresh tortillas? I make the little fat ones, gorditas. Muy buenas," she said, gesturing with her hands. "I am good at ironing, too, señora, for the love of God ... por el amor de Dios."

She was begging and I felt her shame.

Mama stood silently on the other side of the screen, staring at her.

Olga, uncomfortable with the silent stare, said, "Forgive me, señora. I didn't mean to bother you." She turned to leave.

Mama said, "I may have some ironing for you later in the week. Can you come back on Wednesday?"

"Yes, señora, of course I can come back. God bless you, señora."

"Very well, let's see how good you are at ironing . . . and leave me the tablecloth. I have a shower to go to on Saturday." Mama pulled some old crumpled bills from her apron pocket and gave them to Olga.

Olga smiled a golden, semi-toothless smile.

She came back the following Wednesday and never left our house again except on Saturdays, when she would spend the night with her brother and his family.

Olga was like Gaetan, a homeless creature who needed food and shelter.

I don't remember when I started loving that old woman with the toothless smile. But I do remember that when I was young and fell down or got hurt, Olga and Mama recited a Mexican nursery rhyme as they rubbed the injured spot. As if by magic, I would pull away from them, still hoping they would finish the spell before I finally pulled myself free. It went like this:

Sana, sana, colita de rana
Si no sanas ahora, sanarás mañana.

Heal, heal, little frog tail.
If you don't heal today, you will heal tomorrow.

Now my mother was dead. I realized I was crying and Olga was behind me, rubbing my shoulder. "There, there, mi niño," she said, affectionately addressing me as her boy. The tears streamed down my face uncontrollably. It hurt in the spot that remembered Olga, her constant loyalty to my mother and her affection for a young boy, the bastard son of an Indian woman.

Doña Chuy, our ancient neighbor, was giving me her condolences. "She was a saint," she said. "I am with you in your grief."

I found it funny that people said she was a saint. "A saint of a woman," they said.

Mama had had two choices: she could be a saint or a whore. After she gave birth to me, she lived the life of a nun and gave up male company except for Teo, Gaetan, and me.

During the 1940s and '50s she had no choice but to dedicate herself to her son, her work at the store, and her dahlias. She had to be more conventional than the conventions of the time demanded. She walked a narrow line.

La India Bonita, as she was sometimes called, was strikingly beautiful and learned the rules of the times well. She showed her worthiness by not keeping male company, by not cutting her ebony black hair and always wearing it in a single braided bun. At first she lived in the solitude of a small circle.

As the town's women realized she wasn't going to steal their husbands, they came to show acceptance by inviting her to bridal showers, baptisms, and weddings, admiring her clothes and her comportment.

She had only one mark against her, and that was me.

Mama and Teo made sure I got the same education as the other middle-class children in Nogales by sending me to the colegio run by Jesuit priests. She raised me with the same philosophy she had for herself, making sure I knew about the narrow line we walked. "Let others show their copper, Cali," she used to say. "We can't afford the luxury."

The funeral hall was full of old people smelling of old clothes stored in mothballs. Most young people had fled to Tucson, Phoenix, San Diego, or Los Angeles.

Don Salvador Valenzuela came to me with his white Stetson in his hand. I guessed he was about eighty years old. He looked down at his cane as he said what everyone says at Mexican funerals: "I am with you in your grief. Te acompaño en tu sentimiento."

I looked at him briefly and said, "Gracias, señor."

Then I looked down at his cane. It was an unusual one. The handle was made of what looked like porcelain, no, ivory. It was ivory. I suddenly felt dizzy, as if I were going to faint, and I looked away. The world was silent again, like when Olga's sobbing phone call cut the sound of the world outside my office window to tell me my mother was dead. I could see, but I couldn't hear.

With the taste of steel in my mouth, I remembered the first time, more than thirty years ago, I saw that cane. "It's ivory," he had said then. The handle of the cane was a white Jack Russell terrier's head with sharp, exposed teeth. "All carved out of ivory," he repeated.

I remembered the afternoon when I first met Don Salvador. We were still living behind the old movie theater on Avenida Obregón. We hadn't moved yet to the house on Morita Street. He was wearing a white Stetson hat then, too.

A much younger Salvador, squinting with amusement, told me, "With this cane I'm going to gash Magallanes's ugly face." He laughed heartily. I remember feeling scared by the threat that the dog's sharp teeth represented to Magallanes, whoever he was.

Looking up now at Don Salvador, I said, "I had forgotten that cane until this very moment."

He looked at me, perplexed. He had aged. He had red spots on his forehead and was bald except for a ring of hair right above his ears. This was the same man I had seen arguing with my mother in our old living room. I must have been six or seven years old.

I remembered my mother and the man with the cane closing the French doors that led from the living room to the dining room. I remembered whispers and a sinking dark gray feeling in the pit of my stomach. The sinking dark gray feeling was back.

I asked him, "Whatever became of Magallanes?"

His memory wasn't as good as mine. "Pardon me?"

"Magallanes," I said. "What became of him? Did you gash him with your cane?"

He still didn't know what I was talking about. He said absentmindedly, "Your mother was a good woman, Cali. If there's anything I can do. You and I met many years ago, when you were very young. You don't remember me ..."

Our eyes met and we both looked down. It was too uncomfortable to look into this old man's cataracts, to see the sporadic balding that looked so much like mine.

"I didn't remember until just now," I said. "You were a good friend of my mother's, weren't you? I remember the cane, an unusual one, you said. Sent to you from Spain. Carved out of ivory."

With his eyes still staring at the floor, he said, "Your young memory is better than mine."

I told him, "I very rarely saw my mother cry, but I remember she cried that day you showed me the cane. Behind the lace curtains I could hear you murmuring. I remember thinking you were arguing about me. But later, when I told my mother I heard my name mentioned, she said that I should mind my own business ... there were matters for adults to discuss.

"I went outside and listened by the window and heard you say, 'The boy has to know sometime. You have to tell him sooner or later. Let me help out a little bit. It is the least I can do.'

"And she said, 'No. Gracias. No.' Simply 'no.' The way she always said 'no' when she meant it. The iron will and jet black hair shimmering blue 'no.' The eyes without pupils, serious and strong.

"Mother always told me that my father died in a train accident in Benjamin Hill, right before I was born. But I knew that wasn't true," I said, feeling eight years old again.

The old man looked down again and fiddled with his hat. I knew by the sadness in his tired eyes that this crooked old man with the balding spot like mine was my father.

Perhaps it was the grief of losing my mother and the thirty-nine years of hearing people's whispered rumors, but although I tried to feel anger, I couldn't. I couldn't feel anything but deep sadness.

I saw that he was oozing with shame, something I could well recognize. Shame was my lifelong companion.

Salvador didn't leave. He lingered on, like Gaetan, with his bloodshot eyes full of "I know I did wrong."

He came closer and said, "Cali, there is something I have to tell you." I waited for several uncomfortable seconds.

I watched him carefully prepare what he would say next. Clearing his throat nervously, circling his fingers around his white Stetson, the cane hanging from his age-freckled wrist, he said, "On Tuesday nights Chacho Paredes, Pepe el Basco, Ramón de la Osa, and I play dominoes at the quiosco in the old placita. Sometimes Pepe brings hard Asturian cider. You might want to come by sometime ... it's like old times."

I looked up at him and nodded. I understood his confession.

When everyone was gone from the funeral home, I went up to the closed coffin draped with flowers and whispered good night to La India Bonita.

I could have gone with friends of my mother's for one last drink or cup of chocolate, but instead I decided to take the short walk home. Gaetan was long gone, but ever since I was a boy, I'd had a love for blue tick hounds. Like his predecessor, Gastón had a remarkable sense of justice and would howl miserably when left alone for more than a few hours.

As I walked past the deteriorating storefronts that now provided a chance at the American dream to Koreans instead of Jews and Spaniards, I passed by the quiosco where Salvador and his friends played dominoes on Tuesday nights.

I remembered the magic of the nursery rhyme.

Sana, sana, colita de rana.
If you don't heal today,
You will heal mañana.

The Ring

I'm so glad you could make it today, Comadre. I haven't been to this café in so long. The service is terrible, but all I want is a cup of coffee. How about you? An eclair? That sounds good.

I don't even know where to begin. Rafael has been acting strange in the last few weeks, even more curt than usual. Barking his orders at me in the morning: "More eggs! The coffee is cold." Treating me like I was the servant while Delia was in the room. She finally cowered out of the dining room like a frightened dog.

Delia was with us for ten years, Comadre. She was docile and kind and took good care of us. Ay, Comadre, I feel terrible. I wish I could go back and erase everything. But it's too late . . .

It all started on New Year's Eve, and he hadn't mentioned a thing about going out like we usually do. The casino was having its yearly ball, and you know how I love to dance . . .

I had heard from Arlene that she and Raul were going over to the Robinsons' for a dinner party, and I would have settled for that. It's worth going over there just to listen to Rosita Robinson exaggerate about her children. The daughter who lives in Canada really just lives in North Dakota. Her son, the psychiatrist, is actually a social worker. The one she calls the major is really only a captain. But her fabrications amuse me.

When Rafael finally called, he simply said, "Dress up tonight. We're going out. Be ready when I get there." When I heard his tone of voice, I knew better than to ask where we were going.

I dressed in the black silk taffeta that he bought for me in San Francisco last year. When I tried it on in the boutique, he said I looked like Jane Russell and slapped my behind. I never know what his reaction is going to be, Comadre, you know that. He's like the gringos say, Dr. Jekyll and Mr. Hyde.

I felt good in that dress. Delia had just picked up my black satin pumps from the Gato Negro Shoe Repair. She helped me tease my hair a little bit at the top and sprayed Aqua Net in the back where I can't reach. Pobrecita, poor thing, she stayed later than usual, watching me get ready, paying me compliments, and saying, "No, señora, no, señora. You're not fat at all. You just have a full body like that movie star, what's her name, the one with the big bust?"

"Jane Russell," I told her.

That's when I asked her to look for the ring. "Delia, give me the diamond ring the señor gave me for my birthday," I told her. "It's in the little crystal jewelry box, the one shaped like a heart."

She looked in the drawer and said the ring wasn't there. Then I gave her the key to the safe behind the picture of Our Lady of Guadalupe in the hallway, and she looked and it wasn't there either.

Then I started getting worried, Comadre. And I looked everywhere, and Delia got so nervous she started praying to St. Anthony. Poor thing. I could just die.

We turned the house upside down, and by this time Delia was crying and I knew the ring was gone. I just don't know what happened. I knew something was very wrong . . . I just didn't know what. Delia was acting so nervous. I couldn't believe she would do such a thing, but I panicked, and that's when I told her, "Delia, the last time I saw the ring was on December 22, when I went to Adelita Irastorza's shower. I distinctly remember taking it off and putting it in the heart box."

I guess she sensed my tone of voice. Her back got stiff and her eyes got real black, and she said, "Well, señora, if that's where you put it, that's where it should be."

She went down the hall and said it was late and she needed to go before she missed the last bus.

I followed her and told her, "Delia, the señor, you, and me are the only ones who have been inside this house. There's nothing else missing. If you leave tonight and I haven't found my ring, don't come back."

Ten years, Comadre! How could I do that to her?

She looked at me just once and said, "Sí, señora," then walked out with her paper bag full of leftovers from last night's dinner and some chocolates I had given her for the children.

With my heart in my throat, Comadre, I waited for Rafael. I was in a bad way, really. I was not myself.

When he walked up the stairs about 9:00 P.M., I had already cried myself into a stupor and prayed the novena to St. Anthony several times over. I just wanted to take a Valium and go to bed.

He strutted up the stairs to the bedroom like he does when he's had a few drinks and he's feeling good. He was wearing that beautiful brown gabardine suit that Sosa made for him, and I must admit, Comadre, after all these years, he's still a handsome man.

"Are you ready?" he asked. I don't know what happened, but I felt a tremendous hatred for him at that moment, Comadre. I wished I could push him down the stairs. He can be so cruel. You don't know that side of him. You smell the British Sterling and it's all over for you, but he can be a mean son of a bitch — excuse my language.

Removing the tea bags that had been resting on my eyelids, I said, "Rafael, I am very upset."

Then he said sarcastically, his eyes narrow and mean, "What's the matter, Maria Luisa? Did the vegetable man sell you bad tomatoes again?"

I sat up on the bed and said, "No, the ring is gone."

"What ring?"

"The ring. The diamond ring you gave me for my birthday."

"You mean the one you whined about for years? The one Daniel's charged me way too much money for? That ring?"

"Yes," I said. "That one. And I fired Delia."

"Delia took it?" He looked surprised, Comadre. Then he said, "After ten years she repays all your coddling and pampering by stealing your diamond ring? I told you she was an ingrate, and you didn't believe me. These Indians have no loyalty, you know that. Well, thank God it's insured. So don't worry about it. We'll get you another one."

"No, Rafael," I said. "That's not the point. I designed that ring, and we used one of your mother's diamonds in it. How can we replace that? And then this thing with Delia, it gave me a migraine.... I just want to go to bed."

He brushed the whole thing aside as if it didn't matter. And when I told him to go without me, he laughed and said, "You can't stay home, all dressed up and no place to go. I won't have it. That bore Rosita Robinson is dying to tell you more lies about her children, and I promised Nacho we'd stop by the ballroom after dinner. We have some business to take care of."

Just like that, Comadre. That's how he acted. Of course, I thought it was odd that he didn't seem to care that the ring was missing.

He said, "Come on, get your sweet little ass out of that bed and let's go."

Well, like the pendeja that I am, there I go with this beast of a man. Why do I stay, Comadre? Why do I take all these indignities from this overdressed donkey?

I was distracted at the Robinsons'. Rosita has bought one of those golden goddess chandeliers. The plastic goddess twirls round and round, surrounded by a cascading fountain of water. I know it's tacky, but what can I say? It goes well with the rest of Rosita's French Provincial decor. She swears it's imported from France, but what does she think? That we don't go to Casa Marcus? I was there just the other day, and old man Marcus was taking them out of the box. Right there on the bottom of the box, it said Made in Taiwan.

After dinner we left the Robinsons' and went on to the dance at the Casino Ballroom so Rafael could talk to that little pig of a man, Nacho. Nacho with the crotch that hangs to his knees, cigar and scotch breath, and Grecian Formula hair. He and Rafael had business, whatever that means. I just sat there like an idiot while Rafael and Nacho smoked cigars and talked and Raul and Arlene danced the night away. Are those two as happy as they look, Comadre? Arlene's as fat as ever. She wore her tight green chiffon, and Raul held her like she was Gina Lollobrigida.

I couldn't stop thinking about the ring and Delia and the fact that I fired her. I couldn't believe that Delia took my ring, Comadre. It just didn't sit right that after all those years she would steal from me like that. Ten years is a long time, Comadre!

Arlene noticed I was jumpy and kept asking me if there was anything wrong, but I just couldn't tell her what happened. I couldn't bring myself to tell her I got rid of Delia because she stole my ring. After the dance was over and my hair reeked of cigar smoke, Rafael decided we should all go to La Fondita for a late-night bowl of menudo.

Rafael yelled out that it was "the best pinche menudo in the whole damn town!" He was drunk by then. Nacho and Raul had to help him into the car, but I figured the menudo might sober him up and it would be better if I didn't have to take him home drunk.

Well, Comadre, I was not prepared for what happened next. It was the worst night of my life. Rafael walked into the restaurant and yelled out, "Margarita, menudo for everyone!" and Margarita herself comes over and gives us the once-over. Yes, you know the one. She has big swaying hips and skinny legs. Yes, I guess if you like that cheap look, you might call her attractive. Well, anyway, listen to this. She looks at me straight in the face and says, "Buenas noches, Maria Luisa," as if we're all cut out of the same cloth! She's got some nerve.

And then, Comadre, you are not going to believe what happened next because I still can't believe it myself. When she set the basket of bolillo bread on the table, I saw her finger and I was revolted by what I saw. And I thought to myself, as if in a trance, "This finger full of menudo grease has been cutting green onions and cilantro all afternoon."

Then I lost my composure, Comadre. I grabbed her fingers with all my might and crushed her hand in mine. My jaws locked, and I asked her through my teeth, "Where did you get this ring?" And just like that, Comadre, just like that, she said, "Ask your husband."

I must have blacked out. I don't remember what happened next except that later, after Rafael got us all out of the restaurant and into the car, Arlene sat in the backseat with me and said I broke Margarita's finger. She said I got a look in my eyes like a wild animal and dunked her hand in the hot menudo and twisted and twisted and didn't let go.

Did I talk to Rafael, you say? No, I didn't talk to him, Comadre. What good would it do? I slept in the spare bedroom, and the next morning he was gone. Went to Monterey on business. He left a note saying he would be back in a few days and left the brown gabardine suit for me to take to the cleaners.

Oh, Comadre, what should I do? Should I go look for Delia?

Polvito de Amor

Back to this awful café again, Comadre? I hate this place. But I've
got a good one for you.

You know the little Indian bird woman who sits in front of
La Norteña market, across the line? She sells remedies for all kinds
of problems. They say she's very powerful. I don't know where
she's from. Nayarit, maybe. She's very short.

Anyway, I went over to Emma's the other day. It was her
fifty-ninth birthday. Why didn't you go? It was just a few of us
viejas. I guess that is what we are now, no, Comadre? Crones.
Well, we are still good for something, Comadre. Let's not get
discouraged.

Emma's daughter is already thirty-nine. Can you imagine?
She has a little girl of her own now. She's really turned around; you
wouldn't believe it. She's the one who gave Emma all that trouble.
Remember when she was smoking marijuana and refused to shave
under her arms? Emma suffered so much — one kid in Vietnam
and the other smoking marijuana and rebelling, hairy and bra-less.

Well, she's grown up now and she's very sweet. Oh well, yes, she does talk too much ... kind of obnoxious, but what do you expect? The whole family is that way, bless their hearts.

But listen, Comadre, we can talk about them some other time. What I've got to tell you is much better than that, and you are getting me off the subject. And where the hell is that idiot of a waiter? I swear, Comadre, Mexico is going to hell in a handbasket. All the best people are going up north. He never brought me the sugar and now he's disappeared with the coffeepot.

Okay, never mind the waiter.... Chayito and Nacho Montaño were at Emma's, and I want to tell you what happened. Mother of God, what a pair! I sat next to them, and we chatted about this and that, insignificant things like the conditions at the dog pound and how scared their dog, Honey, is of thunder.

For lack of better leadership, Emma and Chayito dominated the conversation, and I sat there and ate way too much of this dip they make with Velveeta cheese and canned chiles. They call it chile con queso. I swear, Comadre, the gringos are redefining Mexican food!

Nacho was the only man there, and I noticed he was really intent on what we were talking about. It surprised me because men are usually not interested in this kind of conversation. But he wouldn't stop looking at Chayito, Comadre.

After a while I noticed he wasn't blinking. You know how people usually have to blink? It's a biological thing, Comadre. A person needs to blink to keep the eyes moist. Without blinking, the eyes dry out. His eyes were glassy, Comadre. Very spooky.

He rested his chin on his hand and stared at Chayito, hanging on every word. Every word she said he considered carefully, lovingly. She would talk and turn to him and say, "Isn't that right, Nachito?"

"Sí, sí, mi vida," he would answer, staring at her like a lamb right before dying. He sighed and moved his chin from one hand to the other. No, I am not exaggerating, Comadre. I know you accuse me of overdramatizing, but this time, I swear by the love of Jesus, I am telling the truth.

Well, I started feeling irritated. I wore my spiky heels, the black patent leather ones, and at one point I crossed my leg abruptly and kicked him with my heel, right on the shin, just out of spite. But he hardly even acknowledged me when I said, "Excuse me."

Every word Chayito uttered was like gold to him, Comadre. It just seemed sick to me. Do you know how long they've been married? Thirty-five years! Their oldest son, the one with the lazy eye, poor thing, is thirty-four, and they were married a year before he was born. Do you think after thirty-five years a couple could still be in love, I mean love like in the movies, Comadre? I don't think so.

The man was just like a lovesick puppy, Comadre ... staring. Seriously. He would take a saltine cracker and spread it with chile con queso without taking his eyes off her.

She showed us a new sapphire ring he had given her. "Nacho went to the dog races and he said I brought him good luck, so he bought me this ring. Isn't that right, Nachito?"

Nacho, in the same position as an hour before, said, "That's right, tesorito." Little treasure. A grown man, Comadre. Nauseating. Simply nauseating.

I couldn't stand it any longer, so I followed Emma into the kitchen to get some more chile con queso, and her daughter followed me. Emma's daughter was aghast at this brash display of vulgarity. I mean nowadays, Comadre, women are much more educated. They read magazines like *Cosmopolitan.* They would never resort to Indian remedies. The three of us returned with the chile con queso and crackers and placed the dip on the coffee table, and Nacho had not taken his eyes off of Chayito the whole time!

Then it got worse. Nacho scooted up on Chayito like he was going to pounce on her right then and there. He brushed his cheek against hers and said, "Let's go, corazón. I am tired and I want to go to bed." Right there, in front of God and everybody. Chayito got all purple, like an eggplant, and she smiled and said, "Ay, Nacho, how embarrassing, honey."

You know Emma. She was beside herself. Her big eyes were practically popping out of their sockets. You could tell she couldn't wait for them to leave. When they finally did, Emma went back into the kitchen to serve the flan. Her daughter was shocked and said, "Mami, what is it with Don Nacho and Chayito? I've never seen anything like that in my life! Haven't they been married for thirty-five years?"

"Yes, hija. But Nacho was having this problem, you know, a man problem, and Chayito was very frustrated. He was depressed about it and she was too. Women our age aren't supposed to talk about it, but she wasn't ready to throw in the towel, if you catch my meaning."

"Didn't they go to the doctor?"

"You know American doctors, hija. They don't know anything about those things. They told him it was nerves and not to worry and charged him forty-five dollars. So Chayito went down to the Indian women who sit in front of La Norteña, and she found this bird woman who sells potions and powders for all kinds of ailments. She bought this little powder called polvito de amor. The bird woman told her to be careful with the powder, that it was a strong dose, and to give him just a little pinch at a time. But Chayito was desperate, and she used the whole thing and then, after a few days, went back for more. And holy Jesus, if it didn't work!"

Emma took a long, deep breath and kept going and told us the worst part, Comadre. The man is completely obsessed with his wife of thirty-five years and won't let her out of his sight! You should have seen the way he hangs on her. He calls her mi vida, my life, mi tesoro, my treasure, corazón de melón. Heart of melon! Like the song! Can you imagine such a thing? He stares at her at night when she's sleeping, and sighs and sighs so much he wakes her up! He wants to hold her all the time now and doesn't let her go out alone. She begged him to let her go play canasta with us the other day, and he relented but waited outside the house on the porch. The whole time we were playing canasta, Nacho was waiting on the porch, all alone in the dark.

So there you have it, Comadre. Apparently this thing with Nacho has been going on for about three months now, and Chayito can't find the bird woman who sold her the powder. They say she went back to Nayarit to get some more birds. But who knows? She may never be back. And in the meantime Chayito wants the spell reversed. Comadre, all she wanted was a little attention, and look what happened! No, I tell you. You have to watch it with those Indian remedies! It's just like the fertility pills they gave Clarisa Choza in Tucson. She had three babies and she only wanted one!

When Emma finished telling us the whole story, her daughter said, "Mother, this can't be true. A little powder can't do this."

But you could tell the girl was curious, Comadre ... she kept asking Emma questions. "Where else can you get these remedies?" and "What are you supposed to mix the powder with?"

Well, come to find out, Comadre, that Emma's daughter married a man who doesn't pay attention to her either, and they've only been married seven years. All he cares about is baseball. Isn't that odd, Comadre? Baseball. A grown man?

I don't know, maybe the bird woman has something for that too. She's just a tiny little thing, but they say she's very powerful.

La Casa Chica

I saw Celina Martinez at Kory's Boutique the other day. She's lost
ten pounds. She's on that chocolate milkshake diet. Yes, chocolate
milkshake. Believe it, Comadre. They're running the commercial
on the Tucson channel. That's one advantage of living on the
border. You get to try all the latest gringo inventions as soon as
they hit the streets.

You have a chocolate milkshake for breakfast, another one
for lunch, and a regular dinner. Twenty pounds in four weeks,
guaranteed!

She's changing her whole look, Comadre. I mean her whole
look. From her hair to her toenail polish.

Remember I told you her husband, Humberto, has been
married two other times? That man doesn't last married more than
seven years! Well, they are coming to their seventh anniversary,
and she's scared he'll get alborotado. The gringos call it the seven-
year itch. One of the spouses gets in heat and starts looking for
another mate. Some say it's a macho thing, but I think our men

have gotten a bad rap, Comadre. I think it's an international phenomenon. The French do it all the time.

But the Mexicans, Comadre! The Mexicans have refined it to an institution. La Casa Chica, they call it. What do you mean you've never heard of La Casa Chica? I swear you chicanas, you've lost your roots, mujer. You are letting the culture slip through your fingers. You have to keep track of these things, Comadre.

Let me tell you how it is. La Casa Chica is when the man — and he has to have money to do this — sets up house for his mistress. Presumably the house is smaller than his legitimate wife's house. That's why they call it La Casa Chica, the small house.

My father-in-law, may God forgive him, did it for years. My old man still gets mad about it, and his father is already ninety years old! A whole pinche family of little kids he had with this other woman. Six of them. Very dark skin, poor things.

Can you imagine setting up a separate house, Comadre? What would you do if you could set up a separate house, eh?

If I could set up a separate house, I would decorate it Japanese style, Comadre, with those paper screens and pillows on the floor. You would have to take your shoes off before you came in.

But I sure as hell wouldn't want another man in it, and I sure as hell wouldn't want a whole new set of kids in it either! I could play rancheras full blast on the radio, and no one could say one damn thing about it. I would shoot that pinche television. Well, maybe I would put it in the closet and take it out for my novela.

Think about it, Comadre. How would you want it to be? But we women don't have those kinds of choices, do we? We couldn't keep a man in a separate house and call it La Casa Chica — or La Casa Grande, for that matter. It's out of the question. Women's lib or no women's lib, it wouldn't happen in a million years.

No, Comadre, we've got the womb and the tits, but we don't have a hell of a lot of choices.

I'm being vulgar, Comadre? And since when were you such a tight ass, anyway? Don't tell me that professional women's club is having an ill effect on your sense of humor!

In the United States the men don't have this Casa Chica business. Not as much, anyway. Only rich old farts can afford it. It's too expensive for the rest of them. They have to settle for a less expensive form of deception.

Yes, I heard about César and Luli. But César has that chain of tire stores. He can afford it. Tu Papi Tires has been good to César.

And do you know how that poor pendeja found out about the other woman and her Casa Chica?

Through the maid! Blessed Virgin, how humiliating! It turns out that Luli's maid and César's woman's maid are cousins! It's a small world, no?

He set her up in those new apartments on Nelson Street. Wall-to-wall carpeting, garbage disposal, automatic dishwasher, the whole show.

You ask what kind of woman would do that, Comadre? I understand both sides. I do. Look at poor Güera, the one who works in the men's department at Capin's. She's a lonely woman, Comadre. She can't even have children. I bowl with her on Thursdays. She tells me things. She's a good woman, Comadre.

And the comandante takes care of her. You should see the jewels he buys her. She was wearing a diamond and ruby bowling pin on her bowling shirt the other day. Real diamonds, no fooling.

My old man, poor bastard, doesn't even know when my birthday is! He wouldn't have the sense to buy me a piece of jewelry!

Who knows? Maybe these women who go for La Casa Chica

are better off than we are, Comadre. No snoring to put up with. No dirty underwear to pick up in the bathroom. They come to you in a good mood because they're not mad at you. They're mad at their wives.

Güera fixes an early candlelight dinner for the comandante every evening. He watches the news. Sometimes they have sex. Then he goes home to his wife and children. Everybody knows about it. Güera has a jewel of a little house ... straight out of *House Beautiful.*

I just think it's funny how she always calls him El Comandante! I mean, doesn't he have a name? He never takes off his uniform either! I have never seen him in civilian clothes, and he just works at the border crossing.

But tell me the truth, Comadre, don't you feel like stepping out on your Gordo once in a while? Don't tell me it's not tempting. Yes, we are respectable married women, you and I. But it's tempting, chingado. Let's face it!

Well, anyway, Celina was buying out the store at Kory's. Everything in golds and greens, fall colors.

How mean you are! She won't look like a June bug in those colors if she dyes her hair a different color! I overheard her telling the salesclerk she was on her way to Berta's Beauty Salon that very afternoon. Copper, she said she was going to dye it.

She's going to give her old wardrobe to her sister and start all over! Now, doesn't that sound like fun, Comadre? It was Humberto's anniversary gift.

"We're going to Las Vegas for our anniversary," she said, "and we're going to get remarried at one of those cute little chapels they have there."

She joked about how Humberto is used to getting married every seven years and they didn't want to break tradition.

"He's getting a new woman, all right," she said, laughing. You know what I thought when she said that, Comadre? Good for her. It can't hurt. Not as much as when they forget your birthday altogether.

And not as much as La Casa Chica....

El Bebé del Vaquerón

Vaquerón's baby was born in Doña Olga Martin's washroom next to the kitchen. The girl didn't know much about being pregnant, so she didn't know the baby could just come out. Doña Olga delivered the baby right there on the spot, wrapped him in towels, settled the girl in the spare bedroom, and went to Capin's Department Store to buy a package of diapers, some baby undershirts, and one of those little terry-cloth outfits with feet.

When she returned, the girl was still holding her baby tightly. The baby was peacefully asleep. The girl was crying.

To see her, Doña Olga felt betrayed herself. To muster up the courage to ask what was clearly none of her business, she drank tequila straight out of the bottle earlier in the day than usual. She asked the girl, "Who did this to you, little one?"

The girl told her. It was Señor de la Peña. She cleaned their house on Tuesdays. He forced himself on her, she said.

Doña Olga, full of rage and the kind of courage that you get only from drinking tequila in the morning, called the de la Peña household. She groggily told Doña Teresa de la Peña, "The girl just gave birth to a bastard son of your worthless husband." Teresa de la Peña hung up on her.

They call him El Vaquerón because he is a cowboy and he's big. He's strong and dark and good with horses and women. Ranch girls are his specialty, but he's not that particular as long as they are young.

Neli was the girl who came to clean the de la Peña house on Tuesdays while his wife, Teresa, had her hair and nails done at Berta's Salon of Beauty, and that suited him just fine.

After the birth Neli stayed at Doña Olga's for three days. Doña Olga said she was sorry but she couldn't have Neli come to clean anymore. It was too complicated. She had already embarrassed Teresa de la Peña by calling her to give her the news about the baby. She could never go to Berta's Salon of Beauty on Tuesdays again.

On Thursday Doña Olga's chauffeur, Fernando, drove Neli back across the border to the Mexican side of the line. He didn't drive up the cobblestone hill. He dropped her off at the corner in front of Cafeteria Leo's.

Neli couldn't go to the de la Peñas' on Tuesdays again and couldn't go to Doña Olga's on Mondays either. She gained a baby and lost two jobs.

Neli's mother didn't know what to say when she saw Neli coming up the steep hill with a baby wrapped up in a white towel. She had been worried for the last three days, wondering why Neli hadn't come home. Neli usually let her mother know if Doña Olga needed her to stay a few more days.

She had noticed Neli was gaining weight but thought for sure it was all the pumpkin empanadas that Neli ate, pretending to sell them to the neighbors.

When Neli's father, Patricio, came home late that night, the first night she was home with her baby, he asked the same question Doña Olga had asked three days earlier. "Who did this to you, little one?"

With the courage that comes only from drinking tequila in the afternoon, he looked in the bottom drawer of the dresser for the Smith and Wesson.

Just down the hill at the Molino Rojo Bar, El Vaquerón was drinking with his ranch hands and playing pool in the dark, fermented hall. Instantly the coolness of a freshly mopped floor and the smell of years of spilled liquor hit Patricio's hot face as he entered through the double doors of the bar. He felt like the Cisco Kid.

El Vaquerón had known Patricio for years. He never knew he had a daughter. After a long day's work they often played pool together at the Molino Rojo, joking and howling at the women passing on the sidewalk.

El Vaquerón only knew Patricio was a good ranch hand, worked for Don Leopoldo for years at the Tres Hermanas Ranch just outside Nogales.

"I didn't know she was your daughter," he said when Patricio told him why he was pointing the gun at him. But Patricio didn't care. He shot him right there on the spot, almost killed him, but as often happens with tequila in the afternoon, missed his heart.

It's been four months now. Neli named her baby after her father. She helps her mother sew for the neighborhood fat ladies who can't find ready-to-wear dresses at the store. She makes pumpkin empanadas. She packs them in a basket and walks down the hill to the church every day for the seven o'clock mass. She sells some of them.

On Tuesday afternoons she puts her baby boy in her rebozo and goes down the street to the jailhouse to visit her father.

Size Does Matter

As if reciting a mantra, Laura whispered to herself, "He was always ashamed of the size of his penis, and he was particularly concerned with how much it weighed." This is what Laura repeated to herself over and over as she got dressed in the tiny bathroom in her postage-stamp-size attic apartment in Cambridge, Massachusetts, as she called her white cat to put him inside before she went to work, as she shopped for groceries or went about her other daily activities. This is what she reassured herself with when she tried to understand why Tomás had left her. There was no other explanation.

She loved Tomás and had tried to do everything right. She was a great cook, loved to read, bought him beautiful clothes so he could show off his strong and slender body, was sweet and affectionate, and was kind enough never to make any disparaging remarks about how genuinely small his penis was.

They had been married for eight years, and during that time their lovemaking was consistent, if not passionate. Although her experience with penises was somewhat limited (she had encountered only three or four in her lifetime), Tomás's penis was small in comparison to the others, but she never said a word. If not genuinely satisfied with Tomás, she had been content. The latest lapse in his libido did not cause her alarm. She figured he was feeling frustrated again, and so she just left the matter alone.

In retrospect, as she tried to make sense of Tomás's sudden departure, Laura remembered remarks he would make in jest after they made love: "Who says it's form over function?" or "Foreplay is my forté." She might have laughed but suspected it would not be the right thing to do, so she did what Laura did well: she kept quiet. Then he would get blue and withdrawn and fall asleep with his back toward her. Laura would press her body against his and say softly to the back of his neck, "Good night, Tomás. I love you." She was not much on gushing out reassurances. She was the quiet type. Knowing he felt insecure but not knowing what to say, she alternated with "It was nice, Tomás."

Laura was from Providence and did graduate work at Boston University in urban planning; Tomás was from Argentina and, after completing an MBA, found work as the organic produce buyer at the co-op. Laura was delicately built; her porcelain skin, long blonde hair, and large brown eyes made her look like a medieval princess. Tomás maintained his strong frame by lifting free weights at the local YMCA; tall and dark skinned, he was stunning to look at and had a beautiful deep voice. (But he had a small penis and tried to make up for it by giving it lots of exercise, apparently not only with his wife.)

"He was always ashamed of the size of his penis. That's why he bought the 1979 red Corvette that he had to rent expensive garage space for, and that's why he left me," Laura whispered to herself as she folded her laundry.

The way Laura found out about Tomás's infidelity was through Pat, the head baker at the co-op. Pat had realized late in life that she was a lesbian. She didn't have trouble now admitting the truth to herself and others—she had been living a lie—but she resented all those wasted years of being with men and asking, "Is this all there is?" This realization had turned her into a brutally honest person. Painful as the truth could be, she didn't hold back. When she had something to say, she simply said it and to hell with the repercussions.

One Friday afternoon Laura was buying a loaf of challah at the co-op. "Laura, I don't know how to tell you this," Pat said, wiping her nose on her sleeve, "but Tomás is humping the new girl from Sri Lanka."

Although Laura was shocked, she immediately knew that Pat was telling the truth. Her throat dried up, and she went home to make miso soup to go with the challah bread.

Tomás came in quietly after work and sat down at the table that had been set for him, complete with cloth napkins and flowers. He and Laura ate their dinner in silence, and the dry feeling she had in her throat turned into doom in her stomach. Tomás got up without a word and sat on the futon couch; he sat staring at the Martin Luther King poster on the wall and finally said, "Laura, I met someone."

Laura was again stunned but not really surprised and thought about "synchronicity," an overused term circulating around Cambridge. She sat and cried by herself at the table. "I don't want to talk about it," she said.

"I think I need to leave for a while," Tomás said.

She replied, "Don't take anything and I won't fight you."

He left that night, packing only his clothes into his red Corvette, and moved in with the girl from Sri Lanka. The girl from

Sri Lanka, whom Laura did not want to name, was eighteen years old, very beautiful, and had dark skin not unlike Tomás's. She wore saris in colors that Laura had never seen before in Cambridge, Massachusetts. The house that Tomás shared with the girl from Sri Lanka was down the street, small, white, and drab; it had a small driveway, a perfect fit for his red Corvette. At last Tomás could park his car without having to pay dearly for the garage.

Laura had to pass the house on her way to the subway every morning, and the Corvette was always there. "Big car, small penis," she said to herself every day. Every day that thought sustained her. It sustained her through the long and dreary winter and the hot and humid summer. In spite of her sustainable mantra, Laura felt numb and brittle. Her existence was as drab as the little white house that Tomás shared with the girl from Sri Lanka.

On another Friday afternoon when she went to buy her challah bread, she again ran into Pat. When Pat asked her how she was, Laura shared the sustainable mantra story with her. Pat let out a guffaw, then her eyes turned tender and she suggested that it wasn't healthy for Laura to constantly think about Tomás and his small and underweight penis, even if it was true. She recommended a grief and divorce group that met at the Paulist Center in Boston on Wednesday nights.

As much as she hated the Catholic Church, Laura was tired of walking around like a zombie, going through life as if in a fog. She knew she needed something and had heard that the Paulists were the liberal types. She had no friends outside of Pat, the baker, and really they only talked at the co-op. She saw no one outside of her students in Introduction to Urban Planning at BU, where she had an assistantship. She hadn't needed any friends; she had Tomás. She didn't demand too much either. Between keeping the house, cooking elaborate meals in unusual combinations, working on her Ph.D., taking care of Tomás, and teaching and reading, she hadn't needed anything else. She had been comfortable and her life serene. But now it was different. She felt discarded and alone, often like she was not really touching the ground when she walked.

She took Pat up on her suggestion. It was almost fall when Laura walked down the steps of the old red church to her first grief and divorce group meeting.

The basement smelled old and musty, and the loud air conditioning was still on. The long room had some exposed pipes and was furnished with black vinyl chairs. Three women sat in a circle of mostly vacant chairs. A middle-aged woman with red hair and pale blue eyes stood up as Laura walked in and introduced herself. She was Renee. Renee's eyes were sad, and she had bags under them as if she hadn't slept in a long time. The other two women were Gloria, dark skinned, with a beautiful head of black curly hair, who spoke with a Puerto Rican accent, and Guadalupe, a stunning woman about fifty years old, whose salt-and-pepper hair was worn in a tight bun. They all smiled amicably at Laura and one by one shared their stories willingly. Laura couldn't stop staring at Guadalupe and her intense brown eyes.

Renee was Irish American and had been married for eighteen years. Her husband, Brian, was "a drinker," she said, and she just couldn't cope with the alcoholism anymore. When their second son went off to college in Minnesota, Renee moved out "without a fuss," she said. She had joined the group hoping to meet a nice gentleman, but obviously she hadn't banked on the fact that only women would come. Her eyes filled with tears and she said nothing else.

Gloria spoke next. "Well, I'm here, girlfriends, because men are scum. I was with Ronnie about six years, and although we weren't really married, it sure felt like it. I worked my ass off and took care of him, paid all the bills and did all the housework. That sounds like marriage, right? Well, when I got pregnant, he dropped me like I was damaged goods. I figured he left me 'cause there was room for only one child, so I said good riddance to the s.o.b. Now it's just me and Crystal and that's all I need right now. Well, I also need a better job. I'm waiting on tables at night right now, and the tips are good but the work sucks. I moved in with a girlfriend and her old man, and they help me with the baby, so it's okay. It's just temporary, though, until I get a real job. I guess I'm here because I feel like killing the asshole and I figured if I talked to other women who were going through the same shit, well, maybe we'd help each other out."

Renee reached over and took Gloria's hand. Laura was growing eager to tell her story. After finally deciding to tell someone about Tomás, she was really ready. She had decided she would tell it very slowly and deliberately, as if she were talking about someone else and not really about herself at all. That's how she would tell it. And she promised that she would not say a word about Tomás's penis. She would just state what had happened. It would start something like this: "On June 19, my husband of eight years, after having a nourishing bowl of miso soup, informed me that he was leaving me for a girl from Sri Lanka."

She had rehearsed the story many times, and now she was ready to tell it and it wasn't her turn. There was a long silence. No one was speaking, and the quiet was getting uncomfortable. Renee and Gloria looked blankly across the room. Laura shifted her weight on the black vinyl seat sticking to her bare legs. She stared at the picture of Jesus in his white robe, his hands folded on the table. He looked like he was getting impatient. "Any minute," Laura thought, "Jesus will start strumming his fingers on the table."

Laura looked across at Guadalupe. Her skin was smooth and olive; she wore gold loop earrings. She was perfectly made up, her lipstick fresh, her long, slender fingers woven together and placed on her black-rayon-skirted lap. Her freshly manicured nails were an opalescent white. She looked fifty, but a very-well-taken-care-of fifty. A red garnet cross hung perfectly around her neck.

Guadalupe reached down to her patent leather purse and pulled out a handkerchief with GH embroidered on the corner. She dabbed her eyes with the hanky, and as she did, two voluptuous tears rolled down her smooth cheek, one after the other. Guadalupe then put her handkerchief to her eyes and wept softly to herself for a few seconds. Gloria and Renee were clutching each other's hands while Guadalupe's sadness flowed out and made the air in the room thick and hazy. Then she spoke impeccably, with a beautiful Spanish accent.

"I'm not sure if I should even be here; I'm not divorced. My husband, Antonio, died six months ago, and I haven't been able to pick up the pieces. It was very sudden; he had pancreatic cancer, and as you might know, pancreatic cancer is one of the most impossible cancers to cure.

"This month would have been twenty years. We met in Madrid in 1970; I was working at the embassy, and he was transferred there from Lima. We fell in love immediately and in the craziest way imaginable, just like two adolescents. I was twenty-six years old and he was forty-five. Although he was much older than I was, we had many things in common. We loved the tango; we were both in Cuernavaca in the fifties, I as a child and he as a young man. Our families immigrated to the United States around the same time; there were lots of coincidences like that.

"Our first night together in Madrid we spent reading a water-damaged volume of Lorca's *Romancero Gitano*, which I had bought at the flea market. From then on we were always together. We were devoted to each other. We never wanted children; we were selfish; we didn't need them. It was delicious to be alone and travel where we wanted and think only of ourselves. After twenty years a visit to the doctor changed everything. He refused chemotherapy; it was a quick and merciful death. And that was only six months ago.

"I haven't worked since the embassy. He wanted me home, and the truth is I never liked to work. I enjoyed my life. But now I feel so alone. I yearn for the children I never had; they could be a comfort now." Guadalupe gently placed her handkerchief on her lap and looked up; her eyes were moist with tears.

The three others sat in awe. There was a commotion coming down the stairs. The Lamaze class was about to start, and it was time to end the grief and divorce meeting.

Out in the street the four women parted like strangers, each going in a different direction down the busy street. Guadalupe walked toward the bus stop with her head down. Laura walked down the opposite side of the street, feeling a lot more grounded than she had when she walked into the meeting. Although she hadn't gotten a chance to tell her story, she couldn't stop thinking about Antonio and what a nice man he must have been. She imagined a slim man, an older version of Tomás with graying hair, probably dressed in fine clothing, judging from his wife's taste, debonair and charming.

Laura found herself looking forward to seeing the beautiful Guadalupe again. Wondering if she had gypsy blood, Laura thought about Guadalupe's classic Spanish lines, her gold hoop earrings accenting her beautiful high cheekbones, and her handkerchief with the initials embroidered on it. Guadalupe looked like someone took good care of her, and Laura felt envy and curiosity. Why couldn't Tomás have been her Antonio? What was it that she lacked that Tomás needed? She waited impatiently for the next meeting. Perhaps through Guadalupe she could find out what went wrong.

Wednesday night came faster than Laura anticipated, and they were all back in the Paulist Center basement, waiting to start their meeting. Renee and Gloria sat together like they were old friends. `

Renee checked in first, relating that she was still resentful that she had given Brian the best years of her life and that even five years ago she didn't have those bloody bags under her eyes and that she was sure no man would ever find her desirable again.

Gloria nodded her uh-huhs supportively and then checked in next. Her baby girl, Crystal, was fine, and she herself was feeling a little better. Her brother from Watertown had asked her to move in with him and his annoying yuppy white bitch of a wife and their three little brats.

Laura didn't know what to say because she hadn't had a chance to tell her story at the last meeting and now everyone was on to the next phase. She felt awkward starting, so she said, "I'm not really ready to tell my story. I'm having a little trouble swallowing, but I think I'll be okay." She was more eager to hear about Guadalupe's Antonio than to tell them about Tomás.

"I finally read some of Antonio's journals," Guadalupe said in a clear voice. All the attention was on her. "I couldn't bring myself to do it until now.

. "I started at the end of the journal instead of the beginning and came to this passage. I wept so much when I read it that I thought it would help my grief if I read it out loud, if you don't mind." The three women shook their heads in encouragement.

"'The cancer is eating me away slowly. There is nothing they can do except extend my life with chemotherapy and I refused. I would rather have the morphine and let the devil take me. I am so far away from my homeland; I yearn for the Mexican sun and blue sky. My only consolation is Guadalupe, my angel. Today, in the stupor of the pain and the morphine, I saw her rise out of bed, her white nightgown glowing in the morning light. I do not deserve such devotion, and my heart is filled with regret that I won't be able to grow old with my beloved.'"

Gloria and Renee were hugging each other, sobbing face to face like two capsized rats about to sink into a cartoon sea. Laura looked into Guadalupe's compelling eyes in amazement and wondered how that kind of devotion could possibly be sustained for twenty years. Her throat was dry and felt like it was about to crack. Guadalupe demurely patted the corner of her eyes with the embroidered handkerchief.

The meeting ended for the evening, and Laura found herself outside the Paulist Center and couldn't remember walking up the stairs. She found her way to the Commons in a stupor. She couldn't stop thinking about Guadalupe. She had wanted so badly to take Guadalupe's hand while she wept. Why couldn't she reach over and touch her hand? Renee and Gloria had become so close in such a short time, but Laura still felt alone and isolated except with Guadalupe. She imagined that Guadalupe's hand would be soft but her grip strong.

Laura tried to shake off the memory of Guadalupe's sadness as she watched the swan boats go by with children and their mothers and grandmothers. There was one swan with a man and a boy. The boy, about six years old, looked down at the water. The man looked away from the water toward the trees. It was close to dark now, and she felt a chill coming up her back.

As she got up from the bench, she started thinking about the girl from Sri Lanka and immediately stopped herself by saying "no" out loud and stamping her foot, a trick she had learned in one of her assertiveness training courses. Wednesday after Wednesday the group of four lonely women gathered for support. Renee was doing much better. The bags under her eyes weren't so pronounced; she was thinking of going to Ireland for a while. Gloria had given in to her brother and was moving to Watertown. Laura reported that she was doing better and was having an easier time swallowing; she still had not given them any details about Tomás or the size his penis. Guadalupe was still wearing black, stunning as ever, and still reading from Antonio's journal. On one Wednesday she read a poem that Antonio had written about her hands.

Upon listening to the beautiful words Antonio had written in praise of Guadalupe's slender hands, Laura lost control. "How did you do it? How was it that you could keep your love alive for all those years?" The shrill in her own voice surprised her.

Guadalupe looked up at the picture of Jesus as if to consult with him for her response. Her hands trembled slightly. "I guess I was just lucky. I think ours was an unusual marriage, un cuento de hadas, like a fairy tale, no? Perhaps the gods got jealous."

Laura put her head in her hands, ashamed of her tears. They all got up and formed a circle around her. She wept quietly and spoke in a clear, soft voice. "When I hear that Antonio died, I wish Tomás had died too. That would feel better than this. I envy you, Guadalupe. I really do. If Tomás had died like Antonio, I could grieve the loss of a devoted husband. I could wallow in the sweetness of grief. I wouldn't have to deal with the fact that he found someone with darker skin than me, younger than me, more beautiful than me. I wouldn't feel so wasted and cast aside!"

Renee rubbed Laura's back gently while Gloria kept repeating, "We're gonna make it, girlfriends." Guadalupe took her handkerchief and wiped Laura's eyes with the expert hand of a mother who had consoled scrapes, falls, and broken hearts.

Outside, the Lamaze ladies with their big bellies restlessly waited for the scene to end. Laura looked up and smiled through her scant tears at the sight of the four of them huddled together while the five waddling mothers waited patiently for their turn at the black vinyl chairs.

They agreed that next time they should meet for dinner before Renee went to Ireland and Gloria to Watertown. They decided to meet at Vesuvio's at seven the following Wednesday. Renee and Gloria walked out arm in arm; Laura followed, and Guadalupe slowly walked up the stairs several paces behind.

As usual, they departed in different directions. Laura had walked two blocks when she noticed that she was still clutching Guadalupe's handkerchief. She turned and ran toward the bus stop, where she knew Guadalupe would be waiting for the crosstown bus.

Guadalupe was sitting erectly on the bench, looking straight ahead in a dignified pose. Laura came up from behind her and said, "Guadalupe." She had to call her name twice. "Guadalupe, I kept your hanky by mistake. Here, thanks." Laura felt she was going to start weeping, so she turned abruptly, about to sprint down the street. "I have to go."

"No, Laura, wait." Laura turned and looked at Guadalupe's beautiful brown eyes. There was a deep widow's sadness in them. Laura stared at the older woman with admiration.

"I need to tell you something. I owe you an apology."

Laura was confused. "For what? I don't understand."

"It's about Antonio. I'm sorry I told you all those things."

"Oh, please don't be sorry, Guadalupe. I was just so envious. I wished so many times that Tomás was more like Antonio."

"It's a lie," Guadalupe said, looking at the street in front of her.

"What's a lie? I don't know what you mean."

"It's all a lie. Antonio. He's not dead. He's very much alive and living with a young engineering student from Brazil." Guadalupe paused and took Laura's hands in hers. "I'm sorry," she said as the bus roared to a halt. "I just couldn't tell the truth, so I made something up. A fairy tale, un cuento de hadas. Please forgive me, my dear."

Laura was as white as a sheet; she was so confused, all she could say was "This has all been a lie? You've been making this all up? The journal? The poetry?"

"He left me after twenty years of marriage. He just got tired, he said. He wanted to start over. He said it felt like his last chance." With this Guadalupe broke down and sobbed like a child. Laura, overwhelmed, grabbed her awkwardly by the neck, and they held each other as they wept at the bus stop. An old African American man who had been leaning on his grocery cart full of belongings stared at them like they were crazy. The traffic noise fell away, and Laura saw the people go by silently, as if in slow motion.

"I just couldn't tell the real story. It seems so senseless."

Laura was still crying as they both sat on the bench, holding hands. She could not remember a time when she had wept so much. She thought of Gloria and Renee and how they both started crying at the first meeting, letting it all hang out. She thought it was because Gloria was Latina and Renee was Irish. She envied the way they let their emotions carry them away.

After a few minutes of calm, Laura handed Guadalupe back her soaked handkerchief. As she looked into Guadalupe's sad eyes, she was still in awe of her graceful beauty. She couldn't believe that Antonio would do such a thing! She caught herself and remembered that she didn't know what part was true and what part was a lie.

Guadalupe and Laura sat on the bus bench for a while longer. Laura, feeling awkward, wondered if she should just say good-bye and leave. Then she said, "Guadalupe, listen, there's a little Greek restaurant around the corner. Do you want to get a bite to eat?"

"I would really like that, my dear," Guadalupe said immediately, regaining her composure. "You have never really told your story. And of course, I've never really told you mine. You were married eight years, no?"

"Yes," Laura said. "Eight years. That doesn't seem so long compared to you. Were you really married for twenty?"

Guadalupe laughed. "Yes, Laura. That part is true. Will you ever trust anything I tell you again?"

Laura smiled. "Is Antonio as good-looking as you said he was?"

"Unfortunately, that part is true too." Then she added with a flashy smile, "But I am happy to report that he has two left feet and couldn't do a tango to save his life!"

Laura smiled and took the older woman's arm. They walked arm in arm down the street toward Papouli's Café. As they came to the door of the restaurant, Laura asked, "Guadalupe, have you ever heard the expression 'Size doesn't matter'?"

Guadalupe let out a very unladylike roar of laughter. "My dear, I think you and I have a lot to talk about."

The Truth about Alicia

The truth about Alicia was that she wasn't that stable to begin with. So when she did what she did, no one was very surprised. Still, it was shocking, the way she followed them from the hardware store to the woman's house, the way she broke the sliding glass door with the tire jack, the way she found them in bed. It was more than she could take, her being seven months pregnant and all. It took only two shots.

It was Robert she gave the gun to, and it was Robert who would have to book her and take her to the station. "Mario's a prick" is all she said as Robert explained that he was going to have to lock her up, at least for the night.

Alicia and Robert had gone to Nogales High School together; they had always been friends. In high school, whenever Alicia and Mario were in a fight and Alicia needed a date, it was Robert who took her to the basketball games. But that was a long time ago. Alicia married Mario, and Robert went off to college. Robert didn't like the university in Tucson, so he came back to Nogales and joined the U.S. Border Patrol. That proved to be too boring for him, all that sitting in the dark green truck, watching families cross the fence. Sometimes he just waved them on. "What the hell," he said to himself as he drank cold orange juice out of a thermos bottle. "What the hell." They would soon find out that where they were going wasn't going to be that different from what they were leaving. "So what the hell. Let them find out for themselves," he told himself. Instead of guarding the nation's border, Robert decided to join the City of Nogales Police Department; at least he had friends on the force and he could be riding around town and not be stuck on top of some deserted hill. Robert didn't figure that his first homicide case would be Alicia.

Alicia noticed that Robert's hand felt just like it felt when he would lead her onto the dance floor when they were teenagers. When Robert pulled her gently away from the crime scene, she noticed that her arm was bleeding. "I cut my arm when I broke the window, Robert."

"I know. We'll get it taken care of. You aren't bleeding too much." He took his folded clean handkerchief out of his uniform pocket and gave it to her. She noticed that it had a blue embroidered R. She smelled it and smiled.

"You still wear Aqua Velva?"

He said yes and looked in her eyes. "I have a thermos with water in the car," he said.

"Robert?" She yelled out, as if she were asking a question. "Robert?" She was weeping now and making her words come out big from her mouth. "Is Mario going to be okay?"

"I'm not sure, Alicia. I called an ambulance. They'll be here soon."

Robert's partner, Olivia Rosas, was in a corner of the dark, hot bedroom with the woman who had been with Mario when he was shot. Officer Rosas, speaking in a low and serious tone, was trying to calm the woman down. "Are you all right, miss? Can you get up?" The woman howled slowly, like wind trapped in a doorway.

It was Sunday, a quiet late afternoon in April; the sun was bright in contrast to the dark house where Mario had just been killed. As Robert escorted Alicia out into the street, she noticed the crowd that had gathered. She turned to Robert, and he pulled her close to his chest. She noticed he was a lot thicker than she remembered. It had been at least nine years since their last dance.

"Was it a wedding?" she asked.

"What?" Robert was puzzled.

"Was it a wedding, the last time you danced with me?"

"Yes, it was Tony and Raquel's wedding. You had just gotten out of the hospital." Robert realized that reminding Alicia of her miscarriage was the wrong thing to say, but the words came out before he could call them back.

"Robert!" It was a plea for help. "I need to throw up."

Robert maneuvered her around away from the small crowd, behind the wall of the house, and put his hand on her back while she vomited.

Alicia thought she would lose this baby too. Right there, the baby would come out of her and fall red on the sandy desert ground, dead.

He wiped her mouth and face with the handkerchief she had returned to him before he cuffed her hands together.

"Is my baby all right, Robert?"

"I don't think there is anything wrong with the baby, Alicia. Now watch your head. I'm going to help you into the backseat of the car."

Robert called in for another car to come and pick up Officer

Rosas and Mario's girlfriend. As he drove away, the ambulance pulled up without flashing lights or fanfare. "Just routine," Robert thought to himself, knowing that Mario was on his way to the morgue.

He drove silently out of Potrero Street and onto Morley Avenue. Alicia laid her head back and closed her eyes. He looked back and wondered if she was all right, but he could see her heavy belly moving up and down. He passed the old yellow building on top of the hill that used to be the high school, and he could hear the cheers of the basketball game, the last game he went to with Alicia. Ten years had gone by. They were playing Douglas. The kids from Douglas would be escorted into a waiting bus at the end of the game and warned not to get out once they were in, especially if Nogales lost. The Nogales-Douglas rivalry was of black-eye fame.

Robert remembered sitting proudly next to Alicia at the game. She was wearing a fuzzy light blue sweater and skin-tight jeans. Her eyes were all on Mario, tall, coffee-colored Mario shooting the basket solo, flashing the crowd one of his famous smiles. Alicia's face would be beaming one minute and suddenly change to a deep, disturbing frown. Mario was flirting with the cheerleaders. They were yelling, "Mario, Mario, he's our man — if he can't do it, no one can!" and Alicia didn't like it. When Robert tried to soothe her, she looked like a caged animal. There was something about Alicia even then. At the time Robert called it a short fuse.

Robert looked in the rearview mirror as they passed the Sacred Heart Church. Alicia was coming out of her sleep. "Do you think we can stop at the Virgin, just for a little while?" she asked in a groggy voice.

Robert didn't see any reason why he couldn't stop; it was

sort of like granting a doomed man one last wish. The Virgin was Our Lady of Fatima, and the golden stars around her head had long ago lost their luster. Alicia was devoted to her; it was this Lady of Fatima who on Alicia's wedding day had received a bouquet of white roses and orange blossoms, a symbol of Alicia's virginity. Robert had to admit that he had been disappointed to find out that Alicia was already pregnant.

It had been ten years since Alicia and Mario got married, enough years for everyone to grow up. Alicia lost the baby three months after the wedding. She became a withdrawn and reluctant housewife, spending all her time with her father and her sister, Ruby. Robert became a cop, and Mario the owner of his father's swamp cooler business. Of the three of them, Mario had changed the least. He still played basketball on Saturday nights; he still had his golden boy grin; he still liked young girls and the girls liked him.

Robert parked directly in front of the shrine on the steep driveway, uncuffed Alicia, and let her out of the car. "I'll wait here," he said. Alicia knelt down before Our Lady, put her hands together, and prayed for a few minutes. When she let herself back into the backseat of the black patrol car, she looked as white as the weathered plaster Our Lady was made of. Then she talked without stopping. . . .

"The worse thing he could've done was go talk to my dad. He went and took my dad out to lunch and told him that he was real worried about me, that I had been making up stories about him and some woman he didn't even know. He told my dad that all he does is work, work, work and that I was like a crazy woman, asking him questions and smelling his clothes. Then you know what he did? He asked my dad did we have any crazy people in the family. Well, that was downright mean. You know my Tía Luz, my dad's sister, is in the asylum in Hermosillo, and it's a big, dark secret that nobody's supposed to know about. Except Mario, that prick, he knew about it."

"My dad came over to talk to me, and he said, 'Now, Alicia, when could Mario have time for all this nonsense anyway? He's working all the time.'

"I told him he didn't understand, that a wife knows, and he just said, 'Mario swore to me man to man that he is not running around on you, Alicia, and I believe him.' I started crying, and he said, 'I can't wait till you have that baby and we can all get back to normal,' and he left.

"Then I got the Visa bill and opened it, and there's a dozen red roses charged to Le Rendezvous Flower Shop. When I asked Mario about it, he said it was a mistake and he would take care of it, but I knew it wasn't no mistake, Robert. I knew it was a lie. Then he said, 'You're a crazy woman' and 'What happened to that sweet girl I married? The one everybody wanted and only I got?' And then I thought maybe he's right; I haven't been myself lately and the sugar levels are real high in my blood and maybe that could make me act paranoid. So I promised I would try, and he said, 'I'm worried about you, Alicia.'

"I was okay for a while until I got the statement from the bank. I never even look at those but this time I looked and found one canceled check from the Silverado Motel Lodge in Patagonia. I just left it there for him to see that I had seen it. He picked it up and tore it up and dumped it in the trash and kicked the trash can across the room. Then he went straight to my sister, Ruby, and begged her to take me to the doctor. He told her I was really going postal and that he was at the end of his rope. He told her that he had been putting up with me for ten years and that I had gone off the deep end when I lost the baby and never was myself again and that the only reason he stuck it out was that he felt sorry for me. He told her that he would leave me if I didn't stop hounding him.

"Ruby said, 'Now what the hell are you gonna do if he leaves you 'cause you're bein' such a bitch, Alicia? Who the hell is gonna take care of you? It's not like you have a job or anything.' Then she got real mad at me and said why didn't I get with the program and stop messing with Mario, that he was a good man."

As Robert listened, he thought about the old black-and-white film *Gaslight,* in which Ingrid Bergman's husband is trying to drive her to insanity. "They call it gaslighting," he said out loud. But Alicia kept on talking.

"The night after he talked to Ruby, he came home smelling of fake strawberries, and I could smell the drink on his breath. When I asked him where he had been, he said, 'Alicia, when is your sister taking you to the doctor? I think you have one of those chemical imbalance problems.'

"Then I knew that he wasn't just cheating on me, Robert. He was trying to make me crazy. And Ruby and my dad believed him, not me. They kept saying that I was making a big deal out of nothing and maybe Mario was just a little stressed out. What was wrong with him going out for a few beers once in a while?

"So that's when I followed him. I needed to know the truth."

Robert saw the golden arches at the base of Crawford Street. "Are you hungry, Alicia? Do you want to stop and get some French fries before I take you into the station? I'm going to have to book you. I can't think of what else we can do. You're gonna need a lawyer, a good one. Maybe Jimmie Espinoza will come down from Tucson."

"I want a Coke. My throat's real dry and I have a bad headache."

Robert drove up to the McDonald's parking lot and let Alicia out of the car. "I have to go to the bathroom," she said, and she waddled out of the patrol car like a free woman.

He followed her into the restaurant and motioned to her that the bathroom was in the back. He ordered two large Cokes and waited for Alicia to come out.

While he waited, Robert remembered that the last time he'd seen Mario alive was across the line at Chemise's Bar, and he was with the same woman who was with him when Alicia shot him. Mario was wearing a bright white cotton shirt, perfectly pressed. He looked larger than life, all six feet seven inches of him. His western boots were shiny and looked new. Mario was smiling his Mario smile as he shook Robert's hand and said, "Hey, bro. What's the good word, dude?" And all that Robert could think of at that moment was that Alicia had ironed the white shirt that afternoon and probably shined his black Tony Lamas too.

Robert looked at his watch. Alicia was sure taking a long time in the bathroom. He wondered if she was sick again. Then it came to him, the bright, tired feeling that he got when he had been up all night, the familiar flavor of rust in his mouth. He shook his head briskly; he thought about calling in to the station for help. That might have made the difference, but then he thought again. "What the hell," he said as he reached into his back pocket and pulled out his wallet. He fingered through old receipts and raffle tickets. He always carried cash in his wallet and one crisp one-hundred-dollar bill, just in case he needed "show" money. He pulled the one-hundred-dollar bill out of his wallet and looked at it carefully. He folded it neatly and put it on the table and set the large Coke on top of it. He looked at the bathroom door and then around the orange and yellow restaurant. The only other customers in the McDonald's were an old woman and her grandson sitting on the opposite side of the room. Judging from their downcast faces, they were newcomers to the American side of life. He made sure they didn't see that he was leaving money on the table. He looked at the bathroom door again, and it was still closed shut. Still hoping that Alicia would come out and he would snap out of it, he counted to ten. He got up and walked out the door.

It was a balmy Sunday evening, and not much was happening on the American side of the border. To Robert the town looked more run-down than usual. Across the thick iron fortress that separated the United States from Mexico, he could see distorted images of cars and lights filtering through the holes in the steel barrier. There was music blaring and horns honking just a few hundred yards away. "Across the line," he said out loud, thinking that at one time it was a mere unobtrusive line that divided the two countries. It had always been so much more lively across the line than it was on the American side. He remembered that when he and Alicia were young, they would freely cross the flimsy chain-link fence to go to a dance, get some cheap beer, watch old Pedro Infante films, or eat tacos in the street.

He remembered that Alicia was once a beautiful curvy girl with black silky hair that reached down to the small of her back. He knew even then that, in all her perfect beauty, Alicia was a little off her rocker. Now she was puking her brains out in the bathroom, with a belly full of baby, a throat full of lies, and a murder charge waiting for her at the station.

Robert got into the patrol car. He took one look back at the door of the McDonald's to see if Alicia had come out, but she hadn't. He drove slowly away.

When Alicia came out of the bathroom, she would see the large Coke and the money and she would know. If she were smart, she would walk the two blocks across the line, take a Tres

Estrellas bus, and never be heard from again. "If she were smart" rang in Robert's ears as he turned left on Crawford. "What the hell," he thought to himself, "they could say she was crazy, but they sure couldn't say she was stupid."

Robert drove down the hill, past the old city hall with the old clock tower, past the Puchi's Grocery Store, past the Nogales Public Library, and past the Dairy Queen. He needed to drive and think about what to say when he got back to the station without Alicia. He needed some time to think, and he needed to give Alicia time to cross the line.

Rat Roulette

Our time in California was pleasant, with few exceptions. We lived in Santa Cruz. Beautiful, pastoral Santa Cruz on the Monterey Bay. We found a lovely house, big and yellow and rickety, in a peaceful and affluent neighborhood. We were surrounded by old redwoods and retired white Anglo-Saxon Protestant engineers. It was pleasant.

Our neighbors drove Mercedes Benzes and BMWs. We were the only neighbors who drove old cars. It took them awhile to realize that we weren't dropping off the maid in our 1973 Dodge truck.

I'm sure that I was the only wife whose husband was teaching their daughter to do Cheech Marin imitations.

I loved Santa Cruz. It was green and moist and cool. It was exactly what we needed after a lifetime in Arizona. There was only one problem. We hadn't been there two weeks when we started hearing noises. Screechy animal noises.

"I think it's coming from the baseboards under the house," I told Art.

"It must be an opossum," he said with some authority. He majored in geology, and so I defer all scientific knowledge to his prerequisite. "I've heard there's lots of opossums in this part of California," he added.

"Aaah," I said, "how cute. Should I call the wildlife people? Maybe they have some kind of trap we can use and relocate it to the woods."

"Good idea," he said. "Why don't you give them a call."

The next day I called the State Department of Fish and Game.

"Hello," I said. "We live in Pasatiempo and there's something living under our house. We think it's an opossum, but we aren't sure. It might be a raccoon or a squirrel, but it makes screechy noises at night and, well, to make a long story short, we're from Arizona, and we need to trap this animal and get it out from under the house."

He listened courteously and referred me to the SPCA, the Society for the Prevention of Cruelty to Animals. I called the SPCA and went through the same spiel.

"An opossum? What part of Santa Cruz did you say you live in? By the creek?"

"Yes," I said proudly. "We live right above the creek." To an Arizonan, to live by the creek is a big deal.

"Well, judging from what you are telling me, lady, I don't think you have opossums living under your house."

"Raccoons, huh?" I asked in my most self-assured voice.

"Nope. Sounds like river rats to me."

"What?! River rats? You're kidding."

"No, actually, river rats are a big problem around those residential areas. I hadn't heard of a rat problem in Pasatiempo, though."

I was in shock. "River rats? As in the Pied Piper? As in the plague?" I said indignantly. "Where I come from, rats live in the desert, okay? They don't live under people's houses and make disgusting screechy grunting sounds at night!"

"They're probably nesting. That's probably why they are making so much noise."

"So what kind of trap should we use?" I asked urgently.

"Oh, I wouldn't trap them. That would be cruel."

"Excuse me?" I said.

"Cruel, you know, here at the SPCA, we would recommend a more humane way ..."

"What would you suggest?" I asked painfully.

"Well, the best way to get rid of rats," he said with the same tone of authority Art used on the opossum theory, "is to play loud music during the day when they are sleeping. That disturbs them and they'll go nest somewhere else."

"Are you kidding me?"

"No, that's the best way. It's humane and it works. But make sure to tell your neighbors you'll be playing the music because the rats may go nest at their house. They should be ready for that, you know, just in case it happens."

I said, "Listen, I may need to call you again, after all this has a chance to sink in, okay?"

"No problem," he said.

I hung up. Now I had to break the news to Art.

"Are you ready for this?" I tried to prepare him.

"¡A la chingada! Rats?"

"That's right, my man, rats. And the worst part is how to get rid of them." I told him about the loud music.

"Loud music? Loud music? Estás loca?"

"No, that's what the guy said. He said that it would scare them away and that they are nesting and that's why they are so noisy." Then it hit me. "Oh my God, Art! They are having sex under our baseboards!"

"I knew it. I knew that if we came to California we were eventually going to run into some new-age fucking nut like this asshole. Loud music, my ass! Who the fuck does he think we are?"

"I don't know, Art, but one thing I do know is I want those disgusting creatures out of here. I think Sara should sleep in our room tonight because her room is right by the kitchen and it's under the kitchen where they have their nest. And what if one of them makes a hole through the bottom of the floor and bites her in the middle of the night? They carry diseases, Art! And they are having sex under our kitchen! We're going to have baby rats running around before we know it!"

"Cállate, ¿quieres? Just shut up and let me think about this for a minute. Don't hit the panic button just yet."

"How grrross!" I yelled, then stomped out of the room.

The next day I had to report to work a little earlier than usual. I had my coffee while the rat family was starting to scurry about. They weren't screeching yet. Last night's orgy probably had them all tuckered out.

"Bye, Art," I said. "See you later, alligator!" I yelled out to Sara, who was already watching the Jetsons in the TV room.

I forgot all about the rats for the day, thank God.

About 5:30 P.M., as I was leisurely driving down to the bottom of the tree-lined hill, I could hear "In-A-Gadda-Da-Vida" playing. It was coming from the direction of our house.

I got out of my car in the driveway, and sure enough, it sounded like someone was having a party. In a flashback moment I could smell the patchouli incense. When I opened the door, I was blasted by two large speakers. They were strategically placed facedown on the wood floor. Four-year-old Sara was jumping on the sofa, rocking out. Art was mopping the floor with Murphy's Oil Soap.

"What the hell is going on?" I yelled above Iron Butterfly.

He shrugged. "It was worth a try," he said as he walked down the hall to lower the volume.

"Did you warn the neighbors?"

"About what?"

"The guy at the SPCA said we should warn the neighbors because the rats might decide to go next door."

"Oh, I see. Warn the neighbors about the rats? Uh-huh, not about the loud music but about the rats. I'm supposed to go over to the old gringo next door and say, 'Excuse me, Mr. Wilson, we are the Mexicans who just moved in next door. We are trying to get rid of the RATS in our house and we are going to play loud music to get rid of them. Yes, sir. Iron Butterfly. We just wanted to warn you that they may not like music and they might decide to come next door!"

He was beet red. Then he said, "So it's not bad enough that I am making a pinche fool out of myself playing Iron Butterfly and Led Zeppelin for the fucking rats! Now I have to go warn the neighbors! You know what? Fuck the SPCA, okay? Tomorrow I'm going out to buy the biggest fucking rat traps you've ever seen! We'll see what the SPCA has to say about that!"

The man took his rat-killing duties seriously. He researched. He found out that rats are very smart and hard to trap. You have to outsmart them, and that provided a challenge.

He began by feeding them for several days without actually setting the traps. He bought Jarlsberg Swiss cheese, peanut butter, and walnuts. He laid out a feast, neatly placing bait for the rats on the traps, all in a row.

He was obsessed. He carefully explained his strategy to me. He called it Rat Roulette. Here was his plan: He would feed them gourmet rat food for three days without setting the traps to go off. He would place the feast right on the trigger but not set it. On the fourth day, just when they were getting confident, he would set only one trap. They could still eat from the other three unset traps. From then on, one of the traps would always be set. Just when they were getting confident, WHACK!

It worked. Art killed eleven rats in two weeks. They were about twelve inches long, not counting the tails, he reported arrogantly.

Every time a trap smacked, he and Sara did a high-five and yelled out, "All right!"

He smugly read an article about the California state capitol being infested with rats. Grown men watched rats travel from velvet drape to velvet drape while they were in session, trying to figure out what to do about the "immigrant problem."

"I could teach them a thing or two," Art said, rubbing his whiskers.

"You're sick," I told him.

He laughed.

"You know," I said, "I think we should get a cat."

"Some maintenance might not be a bad idea," he said.

On Saturday morning we went down to the SPCA shelter to get a cat. We had to fill out a long, drawn-out "adoption application" that asked questions like "Are you going to feed the cat commercial cat food?" and "Will the cat live inside or outside?" and "Why would you like to adopt a cat?"

Art told them the truth. The cat would be an outside cat except when it was too cold. The rest of the time it could live in the garage. Of course, we would feed the cat commercial cat food.

What other kind of cat food was there? And last and most important, the reason we wanted a cat was very simply because we needed a rat killer.

Four days later we received a letter from the SPCA. They denied our "adoption application." They said it wasn't in the cat's "best interests."

Tying St. Anthony's Feet

One day in July, Ruby called from Boston. "Guess what, Ana? I'm moving to Santa Fe." I screamed like a child on the phone.

She explained briefly. Her mother was aging in El Paso; she wanted to be closer but not in Texas.

My daughter, Lorenia, asked, "Are you sure she's moving, Mom?"

I said, "No, mija, I'm not. With Ruby you never know until it happens. Tomorrow she may call and say she's moving to Cairo."

The following week she came to Santa Fe, looking radiant for all of her fifty-seven years. She sported a new bronze haircut, with highlights that added to her golden air. When the gods blessed her, they said, "And she shall take mother energy wherever she goes." She holds people blameless and makes no harsh judgments. She puts into practice the quality of acceptance. Her eyes are gentle and sparkle at the same time. I have never met a person who doesn't love her instantly when first they meet.

With a cup of the blackest coffee I can make, she sat at my

dining room table and looked in the *Santa Fe New Mexican* for a house. She said she was looking for something that said, "Ruby lives here."

Knowing her and her good luck, I asked, "But what if you find the perfect place today and you aren't ready to move until October?" I instantly felt like a killjoy.

She answered, "I'll cross that bridge when I come to it."

She responded to an ad in the newspaper, and we went down to Niñita Street to take a look.

"This neighborhood hasn't been gutted yet," I told her. "It's like home. There are still a few old cars sitting in front yards. Old ladies still grow geraniums in coffee cans and cut up old tires to plant their zinnias in."

We met the Sanchezes at the door. The outside stucco was like chocolate frosting, and I thought to myself, "My Nana should live here, baking pumpkin empanadas with cinnamon and cloves."

We all shook hands, and the energy instantly got frenetic. We were laughing and talking, everyone all at once. In a matter of seconds, we went from where we were all from to how much we all loved dogs.

The landlady, Maria Dolores, told us she was originally from Mexico City. I told her I was from Sonora. She nodded matter-of-factly and looked me up and down. "I thought so," she said. "You're so big."

Maria Dolores was five feet tall and slim boned. People from Sonora are famous for being big and talking too much and too loud. I neatly fit the stereotype.

"Ruby is from El Paso, but she's been living in Boston," I volunteered.

"Ay, pobrecita!" she said, expressing pity.

Don Felizandro, with his bright blue eyes and red cheeks,

was the only native New Mexican. "Three generations," he announced proudly. Maria Dolores told Ruby that she and Felizandro had met in El Paso, adding another connecting thread. "He brought me to New Mexico for the first time in 1952. I fell in love. First with New Mexico, then with Felizandro," she said, flashing a flirtatious smile at her aging but handsome husband. They had two grown children. Their daughter was an artist. Their son was at UNM.

My daughter, Lorenia, noticed the poodle first. Maria Dolores had a tiny toy poodle sticking out of the pocket of her flowered apron. "Oh Mom, look!" she exclaimed, touching the black pompom peeking over the large square pocket.

We all laughed at the surprise. Maria Dolores joined in acknowledging that it was unusual to find a dog in an apron pocket. "But there's a perfectly good reason," she reassured us.

Before we walked across the threshold, she told us about Mojadita, the dog.

"We call her Mojadita because she's a wetback from Mexico, straight from the capital. I felt so sorry for this poor little thing, begging in the streets of Mexico City! I thought she was going to die, she was so skinny. We found her by the garbage can at my brother's house, and so I took her in. We were in Mexico City for three weeks and I told Felizandro, 'Ay, viejo, I just have to take her back home with me. Look at how sweet she is, so tiny and helpless.' Felizandro said that it was against the law to cross dogs over to the American side. '¡Válgame dios, hombre! People smuggle cocaine and heroin with no problem. You think I can't smuggle a little thing that fits in my pocket?'

"So every day while I was at my brother's house, I would walk her back and forth in my apron pocket. Whatever I was doing, I would keep her in there unless either one of us had to go to the bathroom. Every time she moved I would whisper, 'No, Mojadita, no,' until she caught on.

"Well, sure enough, when we crossed into El Paso, the gringo at the gate didn't even notice her. She didn't make a peep. So here she is in the good old U.S. of A.

"And you want to know what? She's picky! Just five weeks after being out in the streets of Mexico City scrounging for left-over garbage the other stray dogs didn't want, she decides she doesn't like Alpo! Imagine that! When the commercials come on and Lorne Greene is talking about how good Alpo is, I tell her, '¡Ya ves! This is a famous American movie star. His dogs like Alpo! But not you! Here you are being picky!' Felizandro calls her a beggar and says beggars can't be choosy, but Mojadita knows we love her. She sleeps on our bed and actually sits and watches TV with us! When I watch my novela, *Amor Salvaje,* there she is on my lap watching it right along with me. Oh, she loves *El Show de Cristina*!

"Look at me! I don't even like aprons, but now I have a whole bunch. Like this, with a big pocket. Just for Mojadita!"

Felizandro said, "Ay, mujer, you've been talking for the last fifteen minutes and they still haven't seen the house!"

"Forgive me, viejito. It's just that I got so excited! The señorita from Sonora. Such a nice family! The little girl is adorable. Don't you think she looks like Carlita's daughter, Amber?"

"The house," he said soberly.

In a cyclone of enthusiasm, we walked into the small adobe house. The walls were pink inside. A welcoming arch led from the living room to the dining room. The kitchen was warm and clean. I could hear the sounds stored in the adobe walls, sounds of pots and pans banging together and children asking for more hot chocolate.

Maria Dolores apologized for the state of the house. "It hasn't been cleaned," she said. But the house was spotless. She showed us the small bathroom and the bedroom. Just by looking at Ruby's face, I knew she was in love.

"Ay, Ana," she sighed, "it's beautiful." My daughter, who idolizes her, didn't say a word. She loved the house too.

We walked outside to enjoy the sunshine. With another sigh Ruby said, "You know, Maria Dolores, I was just telling Ana I was looking for a house that said, 'Aquí vive Ruby,' and here it is; it already feels like I live here! I love the house! Unfortunately, I wasn't planning on moving until October and …"

She was interrupted by another flurry of conversation. This time about St. Francis of Assisi, who was immortalized in a red clay birdbath. He stood right outside the portal by the marigolds, serenely holding a broken dove in his hands.

All I did was touch his bald head and make a whispering comment in English to my daughter, who was starting to look pale from trying to keep up with the rapid pace of Spanish. Another wave overtook Maria Dolores.

"He takes care of all the animals, you know," Maria Dolores said, directing herself to my daughter. "I'm sure he took care of Mojadita when I was crossing the border. Those gringos at the border can be real mean. On another occasion before we crossed with Mojadita, they took the car completely apart. Now you tell me. Do I look like a cocaine smuggler?"

"They were harassing us," Felizandro adds. "They get bored at that job. They're human, like everyone else."

In a flash we were walking through the backyard to Rosita Street. We got a tour of the neighborhood.

Pointing to an adobe wall with a laundry blue door, Maria Dolores said, "The Ranjels have lived here for seventy-five years!

And Señora Montoya, next door, has grown children who come in and out. Oh, and on the other side of the house lives Doña Agueda. She's ninety-five. She needs to be put to bed at night and needs help getting up in the morning; maybe you can help ... you wouldn't mind, would you? Peggy Goldberg, she's a teacher, rents that little studio in the back. She puts Doña Agueda to bed every night, just as if she were her own mother. I bring her lunch ... you know ... everybody kind of pitches in."

Looking over at Ruby, I saw she was in a daze. I started to tell her that houses go fast in Santa Fe ... but instead we embarked on a conversation about how to make empanaditas de carne and lamented about how they are so fattening if you fry them but baking them isn't the same.

It had been over an hour when I whispered to Ruby, "We'd better go." In the whirlwind that we came in, we said good-bye. As Maria Dolores hugged Ruby affectionately, Ruby simply said, "I'll call you."

We got in the car, and I said, "Too bad you can't just rent it now, Ruby. This is a great house, and look at the neighborhood. Who says you can't go home again?"

"Well," she said, "I was thinking maybe I could make the move sooner than I thought ..."

"Yes!" Lorenia said. "Yes! Yes! Yes!"

As we drove down Cerrillos Road, I told her, "You're leaving tomorrow and you have to go to the Jackalope! That's a must. It's just as important as the pilgrimage to Chimayo."

We parked next to the Jackalope truck that proudly announces, "Folk art by the truckload." Ruby made up her mind to rent the house. Lorenia and she named it La Casita Rosa. "We can buy something for the house!" they exclaimed at the same time.

At the Jackalope we shopped for the house. "Let's get some chimes for the apricot tree. How about something for the nicho?" Lorenia found the perfect thing: a pink candle in the shape of a rose, for the rose-colored house, La Casita Rosa.

"You'd better call Maria Dolores right now. Tell her you want the house," I urged.

She looked through her purse for the number. "Oh no, I don't have the number."

"It's okay. We can go back. Let's go now, though," I said impatiently.

We drove back across town. When we got to La Casita Rosa, there was no place to park, so I double-parked. "I'll wait here. Just go in and give them a deposit and tell them when you want it."

Ruby and Lorenia got out of the car and went in. Lorenia came back out to the truck and said, "Mami, something's wrong. They're talking Spanish real fast and I can't understand them. The lady's crying and Ruby's saying, 'No, no, it's okay.' You'd better come in."

I parked in the neighbor's driveway and got out of the truck.

When I walked in, Maria Dolores wailed, "Ay, la señorita de Sonora!" An elderly Anglo couple was standing shyly in the dining room. They looked concerned.

Maria Dolores explained with tears in her eyes. "I have just rented the house to this gentleman and his wife from Michigan. Their daughter just had a baby and she lives only one block from here on Hickox Street."

Ruby was kneeling at her feet, rubbing Maria Dolores's arm. My daughter looked lost.

"Ay, dios mio," I said, taking in the tragedy. Felizandro was silently standing by the screen door, shaking his head in disbelief.

"But how can I go back on my word when I have already taken their deposit and they seem like such nice people?"

"No, no, Maria Dolores," Ruby said. "You can't change your mind. I understand."

Maria Dolores paused and turned to the elderly couple, telling them somberly, "The house will be ready by Monday."

The man from Michigan sighed with relief, and he and his wife left silently through the archway. I smiled at them on their way out.

When I sat back down on the floor to comfort Maria Dolores, she looked at me and cried out, "Ay, la señorita de Sonora!" Mojadita panted restlessly by her side.

We were all on the verge of tears when I looked at my daughter. She was about to cry too. "What happened, Mami?"

I explained to her in English that Maria Dolores had rented the house to the elderly couple, that she hadn't understood that Ruby wanted the house, and that there was a misunderstanding.

Felizandro nodded, approving of my succinct summary of what had just transpired. He added in English, "If I had known that this lady wanted the house, I would have rented it to her, but this old woman gets carried away. They talked about everything except the damn house!" With this he walked outside to sweep the flagstones.

"Señorita," Maria Dolores asked me, "how could I have been so stupid?"

"It wasn't your fault," Ruby said in her most consoling voice.

"But if I had known ..."

"Don't worry about it. It's all right. I'll find another house."

"But you are such a nice family. Look at this beautiful child! And the señorita from Sonora!" She broke down and sobbed.

"Oh, Maria Dolores! The important thing is that we met,"

Ruby said, still rubbing her arm. "And listen, things happen for a reason. Maybe they need the house more than I do. They'll be close to their granddaughter. They seem like good people. You did the right thing. Don't cry, Maria Dolores. Don't cry."

Maria Dolores was inconsolable. "Oh no, how could I have been so stupid!"

Ruby patted her hand. "It's all right. Don't worry about it. You'll see, everything will work out."

My daughter looked jaundiced. With her eyes like large round plates, she asked, "Do you think they could change their minds about the house?"

I tried to comfort her. The tears were welling up in her bright green eyes. "You never know what's going to happen, mijita. Ruby doesn't really need the house until October and this is July. They could live here for two or three months and then decide to go back to Michigan. You never know ... we'll light a candle, okay?" I saw that Lorenia was still clutching the rose candle in her right hand.

Maria Dolores took several deep sighs, trying to fight back her tears. Dabbing her eyes with a crumpled yellow tissue, she said she never asked for a lease because she believes that people should be free to come and go as they please.

In my desire to calm her nerves and comfort her, I said, "Look, Maria Dolores, where I come from we have a little trick we do with St. Jude."

"The patron of impossible causes?" she sniffed.

"Yes," I said, smiling. "Tonight, when we get home, I will light the pink candle and hang St. Jude upside down in the direction of the house. If it is God's will, the nice couple from Michigan will find another place to live and the house will be Ruby's. I can't tell you the miracles I have seen when you hang

St. Jude upside down! Why, we had people moving in and out of our neighborhood, left and right," I added cheerfully.

Not knowing Maria Dolores's brand of Catholicism, I was afraid I had offended her with my joke about St. Jude, but to my surprise she smiled and said, "Well, I am devoted to St. Anthony ... and where I come from we have a little thing we do when we really need his favor. We tie up his feet!"

We all laughed and agreed it was worth a try.

We went outside to find Felizandro moping by the apricot tree. Maria Dolores came out smiling and said, "Viejo, viejo. We are feeling much better now. Listen, tonight la señorita de Sonora is going to hang St. Jude upside down. And me, you know how devoted I am to St. Anthony? I'm going to tie a little ribbon around his feet. You know, tying St. Anthony's feet works miracles!"

"And what the hell does St. Anthony have to do with all this? It's your feet I should tie up and hang you upside down," he said with a harrumph.

"Ay, viejo," she said in an empathetic voice.

"Poor Felizandro." We patted his back. With his droopy eyes, he looked like a disappointed bloodhound.

When we got in the truck, my daughter was green with confusion. Ruby consoled her and said, "Don't worry, honey, things always work out."

When we got home, I passed St. Jude in my hall nicho and smiled. Lorenia said, "Will you hang him upside down right away, Mama?"

I didn't have the heart to explain that I was joking about hanging the saint upside down. "Not now, mija ... maybe later, okay? But here, let's light your rose candle." I saw my daughter's solemn face hold the match up after I ignited it. She lit the candle carefully, still scared of fire.

The next day I drove Ruby to the Albuquerque airport. "Too bad about the house," she said once during the long landscape of blue sky and pale green hills. Lorenia was asleep in the backseat.

"You'll find something else," I said after a stretch.

"I know," she said softly.

After a few more minutes I said, "I wonder if Maria Dolores really tied up St. Anthony's feet . . ." I looked over at Ruby, and her head was gently leaning on the car window. She was asleep too. I remembered that she often said she could sleep anywhere. She looked content and at peace.

We rode silently to the airport and dropped her off. "We'll keep looking for a house," Ruby said, taking Lorenia's hand. "We will find a perfect house, and I'll make a corner just for you and you can come and do your homework in the afternoons. Okay, sweetie?"

Lorenia's smiling face held a quality of wonder I hadn't seen in her ten years. I felt a tug in my heart.

On the way back home Lorenia and I played I Spy. "I spy with my little eye something that's blue . . ." she said happily.

When we got home, the phone was ringing. I ran in to answer it. "Hello," I said, out of breath.

It was Maria Dolores. "Señorita, I just wanted to let you know that all the preparations have been made. I tied three little yellow ribbons around St. Anthony's feet. Did you hang St. Jude upside down already?"

"I was just about to do it when you called," I lied. How could I explain what I knew only too well? That no saint with yellow ribbons or hanging upside down could change the elusive Ruby.

When we hung up, I passed the nicho in the hallway. Lorenia's rose candle had burned down to a flat pink disk on the saucer. With his expression unchanged, St. Jude remained firmly on his feet. I smiled and rubbed my hands around his head to get the stubborn New Mexico dust off. I walked down the hallway to make dinner. Lorenia was plopped down in front of *Looney Tunes.*

Weeks passed with no word from Ruby. One windy afternoon I received a letter postmarked Israel. She said she was sorry but Santa Fe would have to wait ... something about working with children, an opportunity she said she couldn't pass up. I put the letter away in my jeans pocket, wondering how I could tell Lorenia.

Home

The dahlias looked large and yellow on the tuber package. I
planted them in the old wooden planter by the ivy-covered fence.
I wanted to dig in some roots. I wanted to make the house
mine even though it was a rented house. I planted the dahlias in
the name of Quetzalcoatl. The legend says the ashes of his body
were turned into a dahlia after he threw himself into the pit of
fire. I planted the dahlias in the name of my grandmothers who
grew dahlias in their gardens to claim their soil.

Planting the dahlias helped, but I still felt insecure. The rent
was high and the earth shook. I couldn't grow roots as deep as I
needed in order to stay.

The house, like the dahlias, was yellow and big and old and
beautiful. It creaked when I stepped on the wooden plank floor,
and it was entwined in raspberries wild with neglect. The back of
the house hung over a creek and a redwood grove.

I was grateful when Sara and Art found the house. We had
been looking for days. They finally found it while I was in a

meeting on the last day before we had to go back to Tucson to make the move.

When I walked in to see it for the first time, it opened its wide arms to me and whispered, "Home." But the landlord was dry and unfriendly, and he wouldn't look into my eyes.

He wasn't sure, he said. The people who had lived there before had birds and he'd had to do a lot of cleaning up. He wouldn't take both our dogs.

We had to give up our black Lab, Osa. The sacrificing of Osa will go down as one of the things my daughter will forever resent me for. Osa, who couldn't even wag her tail without knocking down furniture, would step on your bare feet and jump on your shoulders but never once knocked Sara over, even when she was one and wobbly.

It wasn't going to be easy, I tried to explain to Sara, to find a house to rent when we had two dogs, one of them six feet tall. Much to Sara's sorrow, Osa was left behind. The Doddses consented to bypass the other five people on the waiting list and rent us the house.

Even months after we moved in, Mr. Dodds would look at me suspiciously when I raved about how wonderful the house was. Art grumbled about the monthly $250 utility bill.

I loved the house. I hung lace curtains in the living room and bought flowers for it. I oiled the wooden floors so they would smell nice when we walked in. But I still felt insecure. Any minute now, with the booming California property values, Dodds was going to sell the house for half a million and out we'd go, I mourned.

I thought it was ridiculous to worry about losing the house, but it was like a mother's womb. Once, at a high point of insecurity, I wrote the house a letter:

Dear House,

I love you. I love that you are big and cavernous and creaky. I love that your windows overlook the wild part of the woods and that the creek roars when it rains. I don't care that it costs too much to heat you and that Art complains. The river rats that take refuge in your cool and damp baseboards and scurry around in the attic at night cannot deter me from loving you as much as I do. Art has become an expert rat killer, and this has awakened the killer instinct in my daughter, who yells, "All right!" every time another creature falls prey to the all-American rat trap.

But as much as I love you, I am constantly in a state of insecurity over how long we will be able to live within your walls. I am afraid that because I only pay the rent and Mr. Dodds is so weird, I may lose you. This worry is driving me crazy, so I am asking for a pact.

I will love you and enjoy you and bake bread and raise my child within these walls. I will grow yellow dahlias if you promise to just keep us in your arms for as long as you can. I am letting go of this worry and insecurity and will live each day as if you were mine.

All my best wishes,

Ana

I took the letter and placed it on the table next to the fresh flowers I had bought that day. The next morning, confident that it had been read, I put the letter in my journal box and forgot about it.

We lived in the house for four-and-a-half years. I always loved walking in the living room. The furniture looked happy. The long hallway, always noisy with the constant flow of Sara and her friends, said, "Go ahead, this is a hallway for running."

When the earthquake hit, we were on our way to the grocery store. We returned to find the house intact but a little shaken. Only one thing broke: the bulto of Our Lady of Guadalupe. Sara and I promptly glued her back together and erected a shrine. This time we moved Our Lady from her usual place in the kitchen window to one of higher honor in the corner of the living room. There we prayed and laid the rosary down and asked her to watch over the house and us. For three days we slept in the hallway through hundreds of aftershocks.

The earthquake shook our souls and changed our course. It was a wake-up call. It became apparent that our roots didn't go deep enough for us to stay. Like the roots of one of the many redwoods that the earthquake knocked over, ours lay on the earth, exposed. We longed for digging in deeper, closer to our place of origin. It was time to move on.

As we looked toward Santa Fe, things fell into place, the steps laid out one at a time for us to take. We started making our way out of Santa Cruz and out of the yellow house. I started feeling a deep sadness. I wept for leaving my friends, my colleagues, this nurturing place.

It was a cold and damp December, and I thought about my dahlia tubers, dormant in the old wooden planter. Each year the yellow dahlias grew bigger in spite of the snails. When they were in bloom, I wouldn't dare cut them until the end of their cycle, and then I carefully cut back the brown petals to make them look new again.

It was time to dig up the dahlias. I will plant them in Santa

Fe, I thought. I will take a piece of this earth, the memories of this house, with me.

So I dug. The tuber roots had grown stubborn with age and wouldn't budge. I grabbed a cold tuber in my hand and pulled, but it hurt. I couldn't do it. The dark, damp earth oozed in my cold hands. The tubers rested much deeper than the depth of the wooden box. I left them there to stay.

The movers came. We cleaned and gave things away. Only the sleeping bags, blankets, and pillows were left in the den, where we would sleep for the last time. In the kitchen, back in her usual place, was Our Lady of Guadalupe on the window ledge. I made a final shrine. I placed an old wooden toy truck next to Our Lady. I placed some gold and red fall leaves collected earlier in the season at her feet and lit three votive candles for our family trilogy. I prayed that Our Lady would watch over our old Dodge truck as we made the trek to Santa Fe. I prayed for protection, guidance, and wisdom.

We lit a fire in the fireplace and went to sleep in the den, where we could see the redwoods swaying in the moonlight and hear the old owls hooting us good night. We closed the door to the den to keep the warmth in. This cut us off from the rest of the house.

In the middle of the night, I heard crackling and smelled something burning. I turned and woke Art up and said, "Do you hear crackling? Is it the fire?"

"No," he said, "the fire went out a long time ago."

When Art opened the door to the hallway, we saw a small blaze coming from the kitchen. "Oh shit!" Art said as he ran down the hall. The wooden truck and the dry fall leaves were on fire. The windowsill had started igniting. Art ran in and turned the kitchen sink hose on and extinguished the fire.

We cleaned up as best we could. Our Lady was intact. We threw the toy truck in the trash. I told Art, "God, I hope it's not a bad omen. What does it mean? Does it mean the truck isn't going to make it all the way to Santa Fe?"

"Don't be ridiculous. Don't start with your old Nana shit, okay? Let's get some sleep. I'm sure Dodds is going to be thrilled when he sees you almost burned the fucking house down."

We went back to bed. As I lay there listening to the owls hoot, I realized I hadn't said good-bye to the house. I got up in the dark and looked for my purse to find a pen and a piece of paper. I wrote:

Dear House,
    The roots are deeper than I thought.
    So long ago I asked for a pact and you came through with your part of the bargain. And now it's time for me to go and thank you for all your years of home. Someone kind will come and fill your space, and children will once again run down the hallway.

I didn't sign my name. I taped the note to the door, confident it would be read. When I settled into my sleeping bag, the house creaked and the redwoods rocked. And to me the owls said their last good night.

Twice-Cooked Yorky

Nogales, Sonora, Mexico — 1969

Chuy Machaca reportedly made beef jerky out of the stray dogs that roamed the streets of Nogales, Sonora. He made delicious burros de machaca, a dried meat delicacy, for only a peso each.

Late-night Friday escapades consisted of piling into Hilda Soto's truck after the high school dance to go down to Chuy Machaca's for burritos de carne machaca. Waiting outside in a cold line, we joked about how many dogs Chuy had to kill for tonight's burrito batch. It made us squeamish, but not enough to head back to the American side to Taco Bell.

Scotts Valley, California, U.S.A. — 1989

Liz and I are waiting to order a hot pastrami at Zonatto's Deli. A lady with blue hair walks in and takes a number from the counter and smiles. She smells of cigarettes and wears jewel-studded gold flats. Her nails are done in tangerine.

As Liz and I wait, she orders half a pound of honey-roasted

turkey and smiles at us again. The clerk asks this kind or that kind, pointing to the different choices in turkey breast behind the heavy glass. One is $7.99 a pound. The other is $8.59 a pound.

"Oh, it doesn't matter," she says. "It's for my Yorky."

She has my attention. "Turkey for your Yorky?" I ask.

"Oh yes. The little thing won't eat anything else. He weighs only five pounds; he's such a kick."

In honor of Chuy Machaca, I turn to Liz and say in a stage whisper, "Where I come from, we eat Yorky."

Liz replies, her eyes dancing, "Yeah, and we pay only three-fifty a pound."

"Turkey-fed Yorky might go for a little more."

We both lose our social conventions and break out in guffaws.

"Ever heard of Yorky pudding?"

"Yorky fricassee?"

"Yorky al mojo de ajo?"

"New Yorky steak?"

"Twice-cooked Yorky?"

Between tears and stomach spasms from laughter, we take our hot pastramis and walk out of the deli.

The lady with the blue hair walks out behind us with her half pound of honey-roasted turkey.

Liz and I stop to read the headline in the newspaper box: "Watsonville Devastated by 7.1 Quake." Farmworkers from Querétaro, Michoacán, and Quintana Roo are living in tents right smack in the middle of town, on the plaza. They are the ones who keep the world magical by picking strawberries and artichokes.

They are in aftershock and culture shock, eating out of donated cans of Rosarita beans and fruit cocktail.

Yorky is waiting patiently in the gray Lincoln town car. He has a special little velvet pillow where he sits as the lady with the blue hair drives him home to dinner.

The Braid

It was only October, and the Flagstaff winter promised to be cold, "one of the coldest in history," the meteorologist said as Ofelia was getting ready for work. Ofelia had arrived from El Paso, Texas, to take a teaching post in the Spanish department of Northern Arizona University. For years while teaching English as a second language in adult basic education programs and Spanish classes at obscure community colleges in Texas, she had coveted this kind of position. She had pulled every string she could find to get the job at NAU, but she hated the cold. The bitter thirty-two-degree reading on the thermometer that she had placed outside her window did not make her feel any better about going out into the icy morning to teach her eight o'clock class.

She put on a Peruvian alpaca sweater over gray wool pants, snuggled up in a cream-colored hat, and took a careful view in the mirror. "Not bad for forty-five years on the planet," she said to herself, admiring her large dark brown eyes, smooth olive skin, and sleek black hair. The air was so dry that her straight hair stuck to the wool cap with static electricity she had no idea could be so powerful. She put on bright red lipstick and gave herself a fake smile in the hallway mirror before rushing out the door. The cold snapped at her face, and she said out loud, "God, I miss El Paso!"

A man's voice replied, "Oh, come on, it's not so bad." She looked back, startled, and realized that her next-door neighbor, Mr. Martinez, had heard what she said. She smiled and said, "Buenos días," to the elderly gentleman, who was busy winterizing the two front windows that faced the driveway. "Well," she thought to herself, "there are disadvantages to having such close neighbors."

The white duplex on Cottage Street was a sunny and large one-bedroom. How a place so sunny could be so cold was beyond her. She had decided on the apartment on Cottage Street because she could walk to the university, the grocery store, the bank, and the Laundromat. There was even a Mexican restaurant on the corner to provide her with late-night dining options. As she walked down San Francisco Street to the university, she had to admit the university campus was beautiful; the tall ponderosa pines and blue spruce made the crisp October air smell clean and fresh. She could get used to it, she said to herself. As soon as she found a network of friends—and she always managed to find interesting people—everything would be all right.

Ofelia opened the door to her classroom; it wasn't much warmer inside the classroom than it was outside. There were already twenty-five eager Spanish 101 students waiting for her. "Buenos días, profesora," they all said in unison.

"It's cold," Ofelia said in Spanish. "Hace frío," they repeated obediently.

After teaching two morning classes, she went home, put her laundry in her VW bug, and drove the two short blocks to the

Laundromat; she took a few papers along to grade while she waited. As she put her clothes in the dryer, she smelled corn tortillas frying. Nothing made her more homesick than the smell of corn tortillas. She thought of her aging mother in El Paso and felt a twinge of guilt and sadness. Doña Angelina was almost eighty years old, and Ofelia felt genuinely bad about leaving her behind at such a vulnerable age. She made a mental note to call her mother when she got back to her apartment.

Shaking off her feelings of guilt, she walked next door to give El Burrito Contento a try. She ordered chicken tacos and guacamole, and they were delicious. She was still licking guacamole off one of her fingers when a young man came by and swooped the empty plate from under her. She noticed his long, slender hands first, deft at rapidly picking up the dirty dishes. Then she looked at his beautiful chiseled face. She wanted to know more about him, even though the young man was at least twenty years younger than she was. Their eyes met. "Buenas tardes," Ofelia said politely. "Buenas tardes, seño," the young man replied. Somewhat disappointed at the greeting of "señora," Ofelia nodded and instantly felt old and maternal.

"I'm sorry," the young man said. "Am I rushing you?"

"Well, I had planned on licking the plate, but I'm on a diet."

The young man smiled and said, "You speak Spanish very well. Are you Mexican?"

"Yes, or rather Mexican American. I was born and raised in El Paso, Texas."

"Well, if you asked me I would think you were from Mexico. Chihuahua maybe."

"That is quite a compliment, young man," Ofelia said, taking a sip of her lemonade. "Where are you from?"

His name was Rogelio, and he was from the small market

town of Ocotlán, in the state of Oaxaca. He and his wife, Lupita, had just arrived in Flagstaff a few weeks earlier, not too long after Ofelia had gotten there herself. It was the same old story: they left Mexico in search of a better life. Like Ofelia, Rogelio was having a hard time adapting to the Flagstaff weather. Unlike Ofelia, he hadn't known northern Arizona would be so cold. He thought all of Arizona was a warm desert.

Ofelia and Rogelio chatted for a while, then she realized that someone was probably waiting for her dryer. She gulped down the last of her lemonade. "Oh dear," she said primly. "I forgot all about my laundry. It was nice to meet you, Rogelio. I'm sure I'll run into you again."

She got up and left a generous tip. Rogelio smiled at her and said, "Gracias, señora. Hasta luego."

As she was putting the wicker basket of clothing into the front seat of her VW bug, she heard loud banging coming from the back of the restaurant. She peeked around the corner of the building to see what was happening. The young man who had looked so serene and polite not more than half an hour earlier was in a fit of rage, kicking a garbage can with all his might. He picked up one of the garbage can lids and threw it hard against the screen door of the restaurant.

A husky middle-aged man with light red hair, wearing a greasy white apron, came out and said gruffly, "If you don't get the hell out of here right now, Rogelio, I'm gonna call the migra." The young man untied his apron and threw it at the older man. He walked sullenly down the street with his head down. Ofelia could see that the young man's chin quivered as he grimaced to fight back tears.

Ofelia felt compassion for the young man and got in her car and followed him down San Francisco Street. As he turned to get off the street and follow the railroad tracks, she beeped her horn. "Can I give you a lift somewhere?"

Rogelio reluctantly got in the car, placing the laundry basket on his lap.

"Where do you live?"

"I live at the Weather Vane Hotel. Do you know where it is?"

"Yes, it's downtown, right?"

"If you can call it that," Rogelio said under his breath.

"I'm sorry about what just happened. Do you want to tell me about it? Sometimes a sympathetic ear is all one needs to feel better."

Rogelio looked over at Ofelia. His eyes were full of fire. His hands were shaking with anger.

"Well, I'm sorry you had to witness that scene. I just got fired. I haven't been at the job three days and I get fired."

After a long pause he said, "I came here because I wanted to better myself, not to be mistreated by fat pigs like that gringo that just threw me out of his filthy restaurant. But as luck would have it, we live in this flea-bitten hotel with a bunch of winos. My poor wife is melancholic and freezing to death. She doesn't even have a decent winter coat. She misses her mother so much, all she does is cry."

As Ofelia drove him to the Weather Vane Hotel, Rogelio told her that the reason he had gotten fired on his third day of work was not because he wasn't doing his job but because he and another Mexican dishwasher were telling jokes in Spanish in the kitchen and the owner thought they were making fun of him.

Ofelia felt sorry for Rogelio, so young and beautiful. That temper of his had to cause him trouble. When she pulled over to drop him off, she put her hand on his shoulder and said, "Listen,

Rogelio, why don't you and your wife come over to my apartment tonight for a nice Mexican dinner. I just got here myself. We'll have a lovely evening and be homesick together. Does that sound good to you?"

Rogelio beamed. "Si, señora. That would be wonderful. You reminded me of Lupita's mother when I saw you this afternoon. I think she'll like you."

Ofelia felt a jolt of old age in her throat when she heard Rogelio compare her to Lupita's mother. She sighed and looked at herself in the mirror as the young man jotted down the address and phone number.

Ofelia did a U-turn and went to Foodtown to buy the groceries for the dinner. She would make them her famous green chile and sour cream enchiladas, and she would cook a pot of frijoles borrachos. She felt cheerful about having dinner guests for the first time. She started humming to herself. Although she knew that inviting perfect strangers to her home was somewhat impulsive (the young man seemed harmless, bad temper and all), she felt like things were looking up.

As she unloaded her groceries and laundry from the car, she noticed Mr. Martinez chopping wood by his side of the duplex. "Buenas tardes, Miss Ofelia. Are you ready for winter?" the old man said, looking up.

"Buenas tardes, Mr. Martinez," Ofelia replied. "No, I can't say I'm ready for winter, not yet. It's only October."

"The farmer's almanac promises an early one this year. Have you ordered your wood yet?"

"No, but I'm sure you can recommend a good woodcutter," she said with sugary politeness. She put her bags down on the stoop and struggled with the key, jiggling it with both hands to get the door unlocked.

"Don't worry if you get into a jam. I've got plenty of wood to go around," the old man said as he went back to his ax.

Her heart softened and she said genuinely, "That's very generous of you, Mr. Martinez. Thank you."

When Ofelia rented the duplex on Cottage Street, the landlady told her a bit about Mr. Martinez. He was a widower; his wife had died of breast cancer in her early sixties. He had grown sons living in Phoenix. He seemed self-sufficient and strong. He was well over six feet tall, a lanky, gray-haired man. Ofelia guessed he was in his seventies.

Ofelia put on some Mexican music and poured herself a glass of sherry as she prepared her famous green chile and sour cream enchiladas.

That evening Rogelio and Lupita were very prompt and knocked on the door at six-thirty sharp. Lupita was a beautiful girl; Ofelia was sure she couldn't be older than eighteen. She was wearing a beautiful embroidered huipil, typical of the state of Oaxaca. The blouse was made of blue velvet and had large hand-embroidered flowers in pink and yellow. Her dark skin shone against the vivid colors, and her long black hair was made up in one intricate braid. The girl was sweet and polite and, judging by her conversation, had had at least some preparatoria education in Mexico.

Ofelia pulled out her Cuco Sanchez albums and played some other nostalgic Mexican music, such as Trio Los Panchos and Agustín Lara. She treated the young couple with the utmost care and courtesy. At one point she swore that Rogelio had tears in his eyes as he fussed over how delicious the enchiladas were. Everything was fine until Lupita excused herself to go to the bathroom and was taking too long to return to the table. Rogelio grew anxious, left the table, and kept tapping on the bathroom door to see if Lupita was all right. She said, "I'll be right there."

Rogelio and Lupita came back to the table, and Rogelio didn't start eating again until Lupita picked up her fork; then he only moved his food around with the fork. Lupita smiled and told Ofelia, "I am sorry to interrupt your wonderful meal. I've been having a little indigestion lately." When Ofelia asked if she was okay, she got very embarrassed and said, "This is really the most delicious meal I have had since we arrived." Lupita's skin looked flushed, different from when she had excused herself to go to the bathroom. Rogelio was visibly uncomfortable.

The evening turned tense after that, and Ofelia hastily prepared coffee and served the flan in the living room. Rogelio took Lupita's hand and never let go. Ofelia wasn't sure, but it seemed that Rogelio was squeezing Lupita's hand a little too tightly. He also never said another word until he thanked Ofelia and shook her hand to say good night. Lupita smiled coyly and made small talk, but Ofelia could clearly see that something strange was going on.

Weeks went by and Ofelia didn't hear from Rogelio and Lupita. Reflecting on the evening, she wasn't sure if she should pursue their friendship any further. She figured they were young and homesick and perhaps not really that well suited to be the kind of friends Ofelia was looking for. Still, she thought about them on more than one occasion. One afternoon she decided to drive by the hotel to see how they were doing. She knocked on their door, but no one answered. As she turned to walk away, a sound like someone bumping into the door came from inside. She looked back, expecting to see Lupita open the door, but no one appeared. Ofelia kept walking down the hall and out of the dark and damp building.

The meteorologist did not break his promise: by mid-November record snows were pounding Flagstaff. So one dreary afternoon, when the head of the Spanish department approached Ofelia with the request that she go to Oaxaca to research taking a group of Spanish students there for spring break, Ofelia did not hesitate to accept the assignment. The thought of leaving Flagstaff in the middle of winter cheered her up so much she decided to stop eating canned soup and make herself a respectable dinner. That afternoon when she went shopping at Foodtown, she ran into Lupita in the produce department.

"Ofelia!" Lupita ran up to her and hugged her. The girl looked pale and thin.

"Lupita, how are you? It's nice to see you. How's Rogelio?"

Lupita's eyes filled with tears, "Oh, Ofelia, I've been thinking about you so much. You are still the only friendly human being I know in this town, and we've been having such a hard time!" Ofelia invited Lupita back to her house for a cup of manzanilla tea, and Lupita told her what had been happening in their lives.

As Ofelia suspected, Lupita was pregnant, almost three months.

"I've been so sick and exhausted. At first I thought there must be something really wrong with me. I thought maybe someone from my village put a hex on us or something."

"A hex? Do you believe in hexes?" Ofelia asked, amused.

"Oh yes, don't you?"

Ofelia was about to start laughing, thinking the girl was joking, but then she saw in her eyes that she meant every word. "Well, never mind that. Now you know that you are pregnant, and that is a blessing, no?"

"Yes," Lupita said with a tentative smile. "I hope it's a girl. I know Rogelio wouldn't be too happy to hear me say that, but

I would love to have a little girl I could dress up. Are you a mother, Ofelia?

"No, dear. I never got married. I had a boyfriend for many years, but it didn't work out. But tell me more about you. How are you doing? Are you adjusting to the United States? How's Rogelio?"

"As well as can be, I guess. Rogelio's had a rough time of it, you know. He didn't really want to leave Mexico."

"Oh? I thought he was the one who wanted to come here to work."

"Not at all. He would much rather live in Mexico."

"I don't understand. He told me that you and he came up here to make a better life for yourselves ..."

"Oh, Ofelia. It's a long story. I'll have to tell you about it sometime." Lupita cast her eyes down, and Ofelia understood she didn't want to discuss it, so she changed the subject.

"So tell me, what does the doctor tell you about your pregnancy? Did they give you folic acid with your vitamins?"

Lupita looked down again. "I haven't seen a doctor."

"What do you mean, you haven't seen a doctor?"

"We don't have any money for doctors, Ofelia."

"But hija, you can go to the community health clinic. They have free programs that I'm sure you'd qualify for."

Lupita confided that she had been afraid to go into the clinic for fear of being deported. Ofelia explained that the community health clinic would not call immigration and have her deported, but the girl wouldn't budge.

Ofelia went to get her purse and gave Lupita fifty dollars to go to the doctor. "You have to promise me you will go in at least to get your vitamins and make sure that everything is okay with the baby."

After some coaxing, Lupita took the money, folded it and put it in her purse. "The other thing I need to tell you, Ofelia, because I know you'll understand, is that Rogelio has not been well at all. He is sick with anger, rage really. Once I thought he would slap me, he was so angry, but he controlled himself and went outside to kick the garbage cans."

"Oh dear" is all Ofelia could say.

As it turned out, in addition to being cold, miserable, and homesick in Flagstaff, Rogelio was upset because his mother had developed a heart problem since they left Oaxaca. He was sending what little money they had left over to Mexico to pay for doctors and medicines. Ofelia's heart was breaking at the thought of this poor young couple and all the problems they had managed to accumulate at such an early age.

"Lupita, I am sorry to be so metiche, but how old are you, dearest?"

"Seventeen," she said.

"You're a child" is all that managed to come out of Ofelia's mouth.

Ofelia then told her about her upcoming trip to Oaxaca, at which Lupita put her head down on the table and broke down and sobbed.

"Listen, dear, do you want me to take news to your family? Can I deliver something from you? A photo? Perhaps you want to buy your mother a little something. I could go shopping with you and we could buy something together. Does that sound like a good idea?" Ofelia realized that she sounded like a mother comforting a child.

Lupita looked up and smiled. "The other day when I was walking around downtown, I looked in the window at Babbitt's department store and saw a red-and-white dress that my mother would love." Tears welled up in her eyes again.

"Let's go now!" Ofelia said in a cheerful tone. "Would you like that?"

Lupita's face beamed as Ofelia went to get her coat. They walked the few blocks and crossed the railroad tracks to Babbitt's. Seemingly without a second thought, Lupita took the fifty dollars that Ofelia had given her and bought an Arrow shirt for her father and a red-and-white flowered polyester dress for her mother. Ofelia, seeing the pleasure the girl was taking in her gift-buying spree, didn't bother to remind her that the money was for prenatal care.

They walked back to Ofelia's apartment in the late afternoon, and it was bitterly cold. As they approached the stoop, Ofelia noticed a small stack of wood by her door. She looked to see if Mr. Martinez was around, but his house was dark. She made a mental note to thank him later.

"Would you like to come in and warm up before you go, my dear?" she asked Lupita.

"Oh no, Rogelio is probably wondering where I am," Lupita said, wringing her hands nervously. Then she said, "Ofelia, one last favor before you go . . ."

"Yes, dear, what is it?"

"Please don't tell Rogelio about the gifts. He would be so upset if he knew that I used the money you gave me and bought these gifts for my mother and father. He's not doing well right now, and I don't want to provoke him and make things worse."

"Don't worry about that right now." Ofelia looked away for a second to collect her thoughts. Keeping secrets from your young husband was probably not a great way to nurture a marriage. "Just promise me you'll get to a doctor one way or another, please."

"I promise," Lupita said as she hugged Ofelia and gave her the gift-wrapped parcels for Ofelia to take to Oaxaca. The girl looked frail in the doorway as they said good-bye.

On an impulse Ofelia said, "Wait, Lupita." She took off her gray wool coat and gave it to the girl. "As beautiful as that rebozo is, I am afraid it is not keeping you and the baby warm." She put the gray coat around the girl's shoulders.

"Oh no. This is too much." Lupita said, crying again.

"Don't be silly! Wear it in good health and save the rebozo to carry your baby when it's born in the spring!"

"Thank you, thank you. You are so good." Lupita said as she wrapped the coat around herself and left.

That night the snow was relentless. To Ofelia it seemed as though she could hear each muffled snowflake as it hit the ground. She was grateful for the little pile of firewood that Mr. Martinez had left; it was burning brightly in her beehive fireplace. The snow made the upcoming trip to Oaxaca a gift from heaven. In her excitement Ofelia bolted up from the table where she had been grading tests and went into her bedroom to go through her closet and see what kinds of things she should pack for her trip to Oaxaca. While she was trying on her walking shoes, she heard a loud knock on the front door.

"Now, who could that be? It must be eleven o'clock already," she thought to herself as she went down the hall to the door.

Rogelio was banging on the door; he was looking in through the glass window, fogging up the glass, looking pale and distraught. Ofelia opened the door.

"Why, Rogelio, is anything wrong? What brings you to my door so late at night? Is Lupita okay?"

"Lupita is fine. Why didn't you tell me you were going to Oaxaca?"

Ofelia was puzzled. It's not like she was keeping this information from him. She hadn't seen him since the night of the sour cream enchiladas.

"I wasn't keeping it from you, Rogelio."

"You knew we were from Oaxaca and you're going there. Don't you think it logical for you to let us know?" Rogelio's voice was bordering on disrespect.

Ofelia hesitated; she didn't know how to respond. "Well, I did go by once but no one was in your room and" — she hesitated, wondering why she should give him such explanations — "I've been very busy." Rogelio was pacing back and forth. "As Lupita may have told you, we ran into each other at Foodtown and I told her then." Ofelia almost said something about the gifts, and her heart started beating fast.

She realized that she hadn't asked Rogelio to sit down, then said, "Would you like a cup of tea or something? Please take a seat and let me make you some orange blossom tea for your nerves."

Rogelio was silent; Ofelia left him sitting on a bench in the living room and went in to fix the tea. When she came back in, he was in the same position he had been when she walked out to boil the water. He took the cup of tea in both his hands. Outside, the snow was forming a white sheet on the window.

He took a sip and sighed. He put the cup down on the wagon-wheel coffee table and reached in his pocket for a wad of crumpled bills. "Here," he said as he put the money on the table. "My mother lives in Ocotlán, near the city of Oaxaca. You take a bus from the central terminal; the buses run every half hour. She lives on the main street on the way to the market. Everyone knows her there. Even the bus driver might know her, and he'll stop right in front of her house. Her name is Clementina Ramirez Quiróz. Her house has a blue gate and a statue of San Martín de Porres in the garden. If you go on Tuesday, you have to go early because it's market day, or else you'll miss her. Tell her I'll send more as soon as I get it."

Rogelio got up and left without saying good-bye. Ofelia watched him go down the driveway, stepping heavily on the snow with his cracked and worn-out street shoes. She felt angry that the young man was disrespectful, but a strange compassion compelled her to want to help him. She knew she would complete his errand for him, even if she felt such mixed emotions.

Two days later Ofelia was on her way to Mexico. By the time she got to the Phoenix airport, she was in good spirits. The sun was shining bright. The flight from Phoenix to Mexico City was uneventful, as was the short jaunt from Mexico City to Oaxaca.

"Al Hotel San Cristobal," she told the taxi driver. Her room was waiting for her in her name. The bedspread was a bright red-orange with blue tassels; she lifted the bedspread to see that the sheets were clean and crisp; she went in to flush the toilet and the water went down without a hitch. "All is right with the world," she said as she changed into her nightgown, plopped herself on the clean bed, and went to sleep.

The next morning she could smell the coffee coming from the downstairs courtyard. She opened the door to her room and could see the tall green tulip trees with their beautiful red flowers; under the shade several tourists drank their cafés con leche. She put on her kimono and slippers, padded down the stairs for a cup of coffee, and took it back up to her room to sip while she got dressed. She unpacked her suitcase and saw that Lupita's gifts had gotten a little scrunched under her clothes. In a yellow envelope next to the gifts was the money for Doña Clementina.

"Ay dios mio," she said as she counted the sixty-three dollars. It was Tuesday and she knew that the rest of the week she would be busy touring language schools and looking for suitable housing for the twenty-four students who would be coming in March. She thought she might as well get to Ocotlán to see Rogelio's mother as soon as possible; she didn't want anything to go wrong. She found herself being afraid of what would happen if she didn't accomplish her task.

Ofelia rode on an old green bus with lots of people who were obviously going to market. Several people got on the bus carrying baskets of fruit, bolts of fabric, plastic mercado bags, and other goods to sell. An older woman sat next to her at one of the many stops. She held a turkey on her lap. As they approached Ocotlán, she asked the bus driver if he knew where Doña Clementina lived, and sure enough, he stopped and let her out right at her front gate. She recognized the saint right away. San Martín de Porres, to her knowledge, was the only black saint in the Catholic church. She had heard that rubbing his head was of particular miraculous value. The little garden that led to the white porch was well taken care of. Judging from the exotic plants that grew in the tangled minijungle, Doña Clementina had a green thumb. As she was about to knock on the door, a stout old woman about four feet tall opened the door. Ofelia wasn't always aware of her own five-foot-eight-inch frame, but next to the old lady she felt like a giant. "Buenas tardes, señora," Ofelia said respectfully.

The old woman looked up at her and said, "Sí, dígame," asking her politely to tell her what she wanted. Ofelia explained that she knew her son and that she had something for her. The old woman's face changed, breaking into many lines, and she started crying.

"Ay, mi hijo . . . ¿Cómo está mi niño? She asked between her tears and sighs. "It is so unfair," she said.

Ofelia was at her kindest and most compassionate, and she took the lady's tiny hands in hers and smiled and told her that her son was very well but very homesick and heartsick that he couldn't be with his beloved mother. Doña Clementina opened the door to her house and let Ofelia into the living room, a room painted a bright blue and obviously reserved for the most special of guests. She had covered the modern velvet couch with clear plastic, but indicated to Ofelia to sit down.

Ofelia gave Clementina the sixty-three dollars and threw in another twenty for good measure. Doña Clementina got up to go to the kitchen to make some hot chocolate. As the old woman stood up and turned, Ofelia noticed her long white shimmering braid. It was the thickest white braid Ofelia had ever seen. It reached down almost to the back of her knees. Doña Clementina served the chocolate in beautiful clay cups with yellow flowers on them. She talked nonstop about Rogelio. "He is not a bad boy, really," she said. "He just has his father's temper." Ofelia made note that people kept mentioning Rogelio's temper. She showed Ofelia pictures of Rogelio in his fútbol uniform and the framed diplomas from the instituto.

After a tour of Rogelio's accomplishments, the two women sat back down to finish their hot chocolate. Doña Clementina sighed deeply and sadly.

"How I wish I could see my son one more time before I die," she said, looking down at the floor. "He was dealt a bad hand. Such an injustice. He really had no choice but to leave Mexico. Why would he stay here if he knew he would be jailed?"

Ofelia was shocked as the old woman kept talking. "I'm sure you, being such good friends with him, know all of the problems he left behind." Ofelia nodded affirmatively, very slowly. It was no use admitting she knew nothing about Rogelio's problems.

"How I wish I had something to send him, something of mine, a piece of my heart!" the old woman said, almost sobbing.

"Oh, Doña Clementina, I am sure Rogelio knows how much

you love him and miss him. He told me to tell you that he would send more money as soon as he could."

"He is such a good boy. I wish he had never left me. But even without the trouble with the law, señorita, there is no future for the youth of Mexico. They have to search for a better life."

Ofelia made sure to notice the comment about trouble with the law, but instead of asking questions that might appear intrusive, she listened as Doña Clementina lamented about the recent peso devaluation, the hard life in Mexico, and how much she missed her only son. After Ofelia got directions on how to get to Lupita's house, she rose and excused herself. "I'd better be going. I still have to make my business calls and get to the schools I need to see."

"Wait, just a minute, señorita. Let me put some chocolate and some chiles in a bag for you to take back to my Rogelio. I wish I could send him a part of me, but I don't even have any of my old gold jewelry. I had to sell it at the market to buy my heart medicines!"

When she came back into the room with the plastic bags of chiles and chocolate, Ofelia was touched by the generosity and kindness of the old woman. "Doña Clementina, please, would you permit me a hug?" she asked.

"Why, of course, hija," the old lady said as she opened her arms for an embrace.

Ofelia's eyes were full of tears as she moved back from the sweet old woman. Then she took the woman's braid in her hands and said, "What a beautiful braid. How long have you had your hair so long?"

"All my life, hija. I have never cut my hair."

"Never?" Ofelia asked. The braid that she held in her hands was heavy; it felt alive and vibrant. Ofelia had truly never seen anything like it in her life. "It is amazing," she said.

"Oh!" Doña Clementina exclaimed. "I know what I can send Rogelio!" The old woman left the room, and it seemed that as soon as she left, she returned. She had a pair of large silver scissors in her hand. "Would you do me the honor?"

Realizing that Doña Clementina was asking her to cut off her braid, Ofelia was shocked. "Oh no!"

"It is the only thing I can send my boy to show him how much I miss him," Doña Clementina said. "Please. I know what I'm doing. If I could cut my heart out, I would send that along too. Please take the scissors and cut if off."

"I'm sorry. I just can't," Ofelia said as she sat down in a pink wooden chair by the doorway.

"Very well, then," Doña Clementina said as she took her braid and put it around her left shoulder. She held her thick white braid with her left hand, and with her right hand she took the large pair of silver scissors and cut it off. She held the amputated braid in both hands and presented it to Ofelia.

"Oh my God!" Ofelia gasped.

The old woman's gray eyes looked at Ofelia with compassion. "It's all right, hija, really it is."

Ofelia still had her mouth open when Doña Clementina said, "Just one more minute." The old woman went to the hutch and opened up one of the drawers. She took a piece of red velvet out and wrapped the braid in it and handed it to Ofelia as if she were handing over a baby in swaddling clothes.

"Oh dear!" Ofelia said as she held the braid in her hands. "Your braid. I can't believe that you cut off your beautiful braid!"

Doña Clementina watched as Ofelia held the velvet-covered braid like a thing that was alive and would slither away if given the opportunity. Ofelia felt dizzy as she tried to walk out the door. The flagstones on the walkway seemed to pop up to meet her step. Each time she took a step, she had to raise her feet up higher to avoid falling. She turned to wave at Doña Clementina, and the old woman smiled and made the sign of the cross in the air, giving Ofelia her blessing. Ofelia walked out to the street and waited for the bus to come. She held the braid in her hands. Outside, the sound of cicadas was deafening.

She walked down toward the center of town and sat down on a concrete bench to catch her breath; she felt as if she were going to black out. "I should eat something," she said to herself, rubbing her head. "This must be what hypoglycemia feels like." She wondered what kind of legal problems Rogelio had gotten into and why he'd had to flee Mexico and could not return. Again she felt compassion for Rogelio and Lupita, so young, so far away from home; she also felt the shame that must come from fleeing your mother country to go to one that doesn't want you. She thought back to the scene at the restaurant and realized that if Rogelio had been picked up by the Border Patrol and deported, he would have ended up in a Mexican jail, or worse. No wonder he was so distraught.

The bus was taking a long time to arrive, and Ofelia could still hear the hustle and bustle of the market. She smelled corn on the cob and decided to go down and investigate. She could get something to eat. She would feel better, she thought to herself, after she had something to eat.

Ofelia was not prepared for the sights and sounds of the market. It was a farmer's market where local growers brought their fruits, vegetables, and animals to sell. She noticed that the old woman who had been on the bus with a live turkey on her lap was now walking around with a bag of fruits and vegetables. As Ofelia passed one of the tents, she noticed that the turkey was on the butcher block, ready to have its head cut off. She turned a sharp corner and went down to where they were selling coffee and chocolate. The coffee vendor called to her: "Aquí gringuita. Véngase pa'ca." "Over here, gringa, come over here. This is the best coffee you'll ever get. You can't get it commercially. Come and smell it! Take some back to the United States! Come on, help me out here. I only have a few kilos to sell and I can go home."

Ofelia approached the booth, took the bag of coffee in her hands, and said, "No soy gringa," as she bought what the vendor had left. She also bought a green plastic mercado bag with an image of Our Lady of Guadalupe on it. She carefully put the braid on top of the coffee in the bag and meandered through the market. She was the tallest person there and had to bend her head to look inside the stalls.

As she approached the plaza, she asked a young woman if the bus to Oaxaca would come soon, and the girl answered that it would be there in a few minutes. Ofelia took a seat on a bench under a massive tree and waited for the bus. She could hear the merchants calling out their prices and taunting the customers. She could smell the raw meats, the steaming corn, and the coffee that she had in her bag. She could see the red velvet cloth that the braid was wrapped in.

She realized that she had not gotten anything to eat, but she was too fatigued and confused to act on her hunger. The young woman who had told her about the bus sat next to her.

"Buenas tardes," the girl said. Ofelia acknowledged her with a crooked smile.

A few more minutes passed, and Ofelia was feeling better, or at least more grounded in reality. So much time had seemed to go by. The market was quieting down, and she wondered where in the world the bus could be. She turned to the girl and said, "What time did you say the bus would come by?"

"Every half hour."

"I've been here longer than a half hour," Ofelia said.

"Sometimes they don't run on time," the girl said nonchalantly.

"Of course," Ofelia said, staring blankly. "How stupid of me," she thought to herself.

"Are you all right? the girl asked.

"I think I'm a little dehydrated."

"They have good aguas over there, seño. You could get yourself something to drink."

"Now I am feeling really stupid," Ofelia thought to herself.

"Gracias," she said as she got up and bought herself an agua de tamarindo. No sooner had she taken her first gulp than she looked at the wall and read a poster warning about cholera in the area.

"Lovely. Just lovely," Ofelia said as she finished her agua de tamarindo and went back to her bench. She felt so much better that she didn't care if she got cholera later that evening and died. She sat back on the bench and smiled at the girl.

"So, are you a student?" she asked the girl.

The girl was friendly and told her she went to the nun's school—Nuestra Señora de la Piedad. They chatted comfortably for a few minutes, and Ofelia told the girl that she had been to see Doña Clementina.

The girl looked sad and said, "Pobrecita."

Ofelia was curious and asked her why she said that and that she seemed to be doing better with her medications.

The girl turned and said, "Do you know what happened with Rogelio, her son?"

"No, I know he had some trouble, but I don't know what it was."

"Well, he killed a man and fled. No one knows where he is. Some say he went into Guatemala, but I think he was too smart for that. They hate Indians even more in Guatemala than they do in Mexico. I think he went north, to Nogales."

Ofelia was flabbergasted. "Oh dear, dear," she said.

The girl went on to say that Rogelio had a bad temper — "muy corajudo," she said — and that it wasn't really his fault.

It happened at a fútbol game. Rogelio was the goalie, and many thought he would play professionally, he was so good. His team was playing their close rivals from Puerto Escondido, and the game got out of hand, as fútbol games do. Apparently the referee made a bad call and the crowd got too excited. Rogelio insulted him and one thing led to another. Rogelio kicked the referee in the head and the man died instantly, right there on the spot.

"Oh my God!" Ofelia said, and the earth spun.

"Here comes the bus now!" the girl said as she stood up.

Ofelia couldn't move. "Come on, here's the bus," the girl coaxed.

Ofelia climbed up into the bus and sat in the back. The girl met up with some of her friends, and they chattered and laughed as the bus bounced down the street full of potholes. Ofelia put the mercado bag on the seat next to her, leaned her head on the dirty window, and closed her eyes.

"Holy Mother of God," she said as she fell into a deep and groggy sleep.

The next thing Ofelia heard was the screeching of brakes and the bus driver yelling, "Central!" Startled, she got up and grabbed the mercado bag, which had been smashed by the man who sat next to her during the trip back to Oaxaca City. She walked out into the street and hailed a cab, went back to the hotel, and slept for four hours straight. When she woke up, it was dark. Too tired to eat anything, she got into her nightgown and went back to sleep.

The next morning Ofelia woke up famished. She went down to the Camino Real Hotel, a beautifully restored Dominican convent with a courtyard full of flowers and exotic succulent plants. A music system was playing Gregorian chants. She sat in a pigskin chair and ordered huevos con chorizo, coffee, fresh fruit, and orange juice. She ate as though someone had her locked up for days. Then she went about her business and found several good places for students to stay and got into the whirlwind of her business trip. She visited the markets and the zócalo and tried to forget about Rogelio, Doña Clementina, and the braid. She decided against finding Lupita's family and got the hotel owner to hire a driver and hand-deliver the gifts. Meeting one side of the family was all she could handle.

On her last night in Oaxaca, Ofelia decided that angel-wing ice cream sounded too divine to pass up, so she indulged in an ice cream cone, strolled around the zócalo, listened to the wonderful marimbas, and took in the balmy breeze.

A day later she was back in Flagstaff with a bad case of dysentery. She put the mercado bag and all its contents in the kitchen by the plant stand. Every time she thought about the braid, she felt nauseated; she couldn't bear the thought of finding Rogelio and Lupita and giving them Doña Clementina's gift.

Several days went by and Ofelia, weakened by her ongoing bout with dysentery, put the memory of the braid behind her. One afternoon as she was walking home from school, she saw Lupita walking up Cottage Street. The antibiotics were not working as fast as the doctor said they would, and she was still not feeling well. When Ofelia saw Lupita, she groaned out loud, "Oh no, I just can't deal with this right now."

Lupita saw her right away, smiled, and stopped in the driveway of Ofelia's duplex, waiting for Ofelia to come closer. They exchanged their usual greetings.

Ofelia started apologizing. "I'm so sorry I haven't been to see you ..."

The girl interrupted her. "Listen, Ofelia, I am going back to Mexico, leaving Rogelio. He just gets more and more out of control every day, and now I am scared of what he might do to me. I think he is definitely embrujado."

"Embrujado?" Ofelia remembered that Lupita believed in hexes. "Are you in danger?"

"I don't think I am in danger, Ofelia. I think you are. That is why I am here. Doña Clementina's neighbor wrote to Rogelio and told him Doña Cleme's very sick. Apparently she got worse after you came to visit. She told Rogelio that you cut off all of Doña Cleme's hair and that after that, she got worse. She told him she thought you were a bruja. Rogelio told me he was going to come and get the braid from you and that he didn't care what he had to do to get it. He can be very violent, Ofelia. If Doña Cleme dies, he'll come after you. I'm not exaggerating!"

"The braid!" Ofelia exclaimed. "The braid! Oh my God! I have it. I'll give it to you and you can take it to Rogelio. Come in and let me show it to you."

As they entered the apartment, Ofelia explained, "Lupita, I was just so upset when I went to Ocotlán and they told me that Rogelio had killed a man. I just didn't want to face him; I was frightened. Then I have this stomach problem that I haven't been able to get rid of. I meant to bring the braid to you, really I did." Ofelia saw the expression on Lupita's face and knew she wasn't getting through. "But you should know that I mean no harm, Lupita. I don't even believe in brujas!"

Ofelia ran to get the mercado bag and brought it to the kitchen table. She put her hand in and pulled the red velvet cloth out, but the braid was not in the cloth. "Wait, let me get the rest of the stuff out of here. It must have fallen to the bottom."

Ofelia rummaged around to get the braid, but she couldn't feel it. She became frantic and emptied the contents of the bag onto the table. There were the chocolate and chiles that Doña Clementina had sent Rogelio and the coffee she had bought at the market. The braid was gone.

"It was right in here!" she said, looking at Lupita as she held the empty red velvet cloth in her hand. Lupita's eyes were round and black, with nothing but pupils showing. "It must be in my suitcase. I haven't even unpacked everything!"

The girl got up. "Listen, Ofelia, I have to go, but please, if what you say is true, please find Rogelio and give him his mother's braid. He is convinced that you are trying to harm him and his mother. He is crazy with rage."

"Wait, don't go! Let me find it and give it to you." Ofelia rushed down the hallway and looked back as she saw the girl walk out the door. She turned to follow Lupita, saying, "Don't worry, Lupita. I'll find the braid. I'll explain everything. Don't worry. Wait, let me give you some money for your trip!"

"I don't need money right now, Ofelia. I need to go. I'll pray for you."

Ofelia was stunned and ran frantically to her bedroom and looked through all her bags and her briefcase. She sat on her bed and retraced her steps in her mind. She was sure she had never let go of that bag! Perhaps she left it in the hotel room. She got up immediately and went to the phone to call the Hotel San Cristobal. They had not found anything. Maybe it fell off on the plane. No. She had put the mercado bag in her carry-on bag. She never opened the carry-on again. She was so sick on the plane that she passed out and didn't wake up again until she reached the Phoenix airport. She took the shuttle to Flagstaff and went home like a zombie. She didn't even remember going to baggage claim. It was all a big blur. Where could it be? Her stomach began cramping again. She groaned and curled up in a fetal position on her unmade bed and fell asleep.

She was awakened by a hard knock on the glass window-pane of her front door. She struggled to get up and wobbled slowly down the hall. She peeked down the hallway and saw Rogelio's dark head of straight hair through the window. He was pounding on the glass.

"Ofelia! Open the door!"

Mr. Martinez came out to see what was going on. Ofelia could see that the two men were exchanging words. Mr. Martinez looked cross. He pointed to Rogelio to be on his way. Rogelio stomped away, and when he was gone, Mr. Martinez came up to the small window and peered into Ofelia's kitchen. She waited until he left before she went inside the bedroom and sat down on the bed with relief.

"Oh, thank God for nosy neighbors," she said to herself. After a few minutes she picked up the phone and dialed Mr. Martinez's number.

"Hello, Mr. Martinez? Yes, it's me, Ofelia. I am so sorry about what just happened."

"Is everything okay?" Mr. Martinez said. "This young punk, he was pretty bent out of shape. He's not dangerous or anything like that, is he?"

"Well, funny you should ask," Ofelia said.

There was a long pause. Ofelia was at a loss for words. She didn't know her neighbor very well. Then she said, "Mr. Martinez, you wouldn't know if there is a good wig maker in Flagstaff, by any chance?"

"A good wig maker? Miss Ofelia, what does that have to do with our conversation?"

"It's a long story. I'm sorry about all this. If you care to know, I'll tell you about it later, but right now I just need someone to help me find a long white braid."

"Well, I don't know about this," Mr. Martinez said skeptically.

"Of course you don't. I'm sorry. Please forget the whole thing. I shouldn't have asked you. You must think I'm crazy but I'm not. I'm really a very stable person, very responsible, really. It's just that . . . well, never mind. Please forgive the inconvenience."

Ofelia hung up. Her palms were sweaty, and she felt as if she were going to pass out from the chills she had running up and down her spine. She wasn't sure if it was the dysentery or her nervousness over the close encounter with Rogelio.

The phone rang and startled her. Her heart was beating fast. She picked up without saying hello.

"Miss Ofelia, Martinez here."

"Yes?" She had a throbbing headache.

"When my wife had cancer, she went to this man out in Winslow. His name is Willie Reason, and he has a pawn shop. He also sells wigs and other secondhand stuff. He used to make wigs for some Hollywood outfit. He's an odd kind of guy, but I think he might be able to help you."

"How far is Winslow from here?"

"It's fifty-seven miles, but with the snow and everything, it might take you a couple of hours to get there. It's coming down pretty hard and they're expecting more."

"Of course," Ofelia said.

"I would wait a while if I were you."

"I don't have much time," Ofelia said, rubbing her temples. There was another dead silence.

"They're expecting up to twelve inches."

"What's the name of the shop?"

"El Porvenir Pawn and Junk Shop."

"In Winslow?"

"Yes, down 180. You can't miss it. It's right on the main drag. Right next to the Double LL Motel."

"Thank you, Mr. Martinez."

Mr. Martinez hung up, and Ofelia sat on her bed, listening to the crows caw overhead. She went to the kitchen and took two Tums and two Bufferins and started the coffee. While the coffee was brewing, she pulled out a road map and looked up Winslow. She filled a plastic bottle full of water and grabbed a package of saltine crackers. She went into her room and changed into a pair of jeans, a black turtleneck sweater, and her snow boots. She grabbed her purple down jacket and was ready to pour hot coffee into a thermos bottle when she heard another knock on the door. Earlier she'd had the foresight to pull the blind down on the door window since she didn't want anyone peering into her kitchen unannounced.

She crept over to the side of the door and peeked out through the crack. It was Mr. Martinez. He had a fur hunting hat on and looked like the Hispanic version of Elmer Fudd. She opened the door quickly and let him in. He was holding two cups of steaming coffee and was decked out in full Flagstaff regalia, complete with red-and-black plaid jacket and oversized snow boots. He handed her a cup of coffee and said, "I have an old four-wheel-drive truck that can drive through anything. I'll pull up in front of the door in case someone is waiting for us out in the street."

Ofelia flung her arms around Mr. Martinez's neck and kissed his scruffy unshaved face. "You're an angel!"

"I'm just curious, that's all," he said.

Ofelia sat in Mr. Martinez's old Chevy truck and sipped her coffee as she looked around to make sure no one was following them. They got out onto the highway without being noticed. It had stopped snowing, and the snowplows had been out just ahead of them. As they drove, Ofelia told Mr. Martinez the whole story. He laughed in some parts and shook his head in others, but overall he proved to be a good and careful listener.

In turn, Ofelia learned that Mr. Martinez was seventy-eight years old, a World War II vet, that his two sons worked in Phoenix for the state of Arizona, and that his wife of fifty years had died of breast cancer ten years ago.

"That's how I met Willie Reason," he said. "After my wife went through chemo and radiation treatments, her hair never really grew back. She was so depressed about it she became hell-bent on getting a wig made that looked like her real hair. Well, she gathered up pictures of herself, and we took them down to Willie. She even had a paper bag with some hair that her mother had saved for her from the very first time she had her long hair cut when she was a young woman. Well, gosh darn if Willie didn't make her the best, most natural wig you ever saw. He matched her hair color perfectly. She was so happy," he said wistfully. "Yep, if anyone can make you that braid, it's Willie, all right."

Ofelia felt safe in Mr. Martinez's old truck. He grabbed a pillow from the slot in back of the seat and said, "Why don't you doze off a bit? I'll holler when we get there."

Ofelia rested her head on the pillow and fell into a delicious sleep. The truck stalled a little when they got into the town of Winslow, and Ofelia woke up as they were driving up to

El Porvenir Pawn and Junk Shop. Willie Reason's store was everything Ofelia had expected. Part taxidermist, part thrift store, part pawn shop, Willie had it all. With his long white hair and whiskers, he looked like a caricature of General Custer and spoke with a twang.

He knew everything about everyone and was not one bit hesitant to share it, but Mr. Martinez got him to focus on the task at hand. When Willie went off on a tangent about the way things used to be in Winslow before the big boom, Mr. Martinez pounded on the counter and yelled, "Willie, this lady needs a braid!"

Willie stopped dead in the middle of a sentence and, as if in a trance, changed instantly. Looking at Ofelia, he said, "Well, first I'll need dimensions."

Ofelia described the braid as about twenty-four inches long and four inches thick. She started telling him the story about how Doña Clementina had never cut her hair, and Willie said, "Are you some kind of bruja or something? 'Cause I ain't down for dealing with brujas. Let's make that perfectamente clear right now."

"I swear to you on my father's grave, Mr. Reason, that I don't even have an interest, much less a belief, in brujas."

"Messin' around with hair and body parts ain't exactly a wise thing to do, I hope you know."

"I understand, sir. Believe me, this was beyond my control. But if I don't produce the braid, I think it is safe to say that it could be dangerous for me."

"Well, never mind. I know more than I want to know already."

With a gleam of amusement in his blue eyes, Mr. Martinez was smiling to himself and looking at the vast collection of turquoise jewelry in the glass cases.

The rattlesnake rattles that Willie had hanging on the door announced that someone had come into the store. A regal Navajo woman about sixty years old walked in. She was wearing traditional clothing, a black velvet broom skirt and burgundy blouse. She carried with her a wooden case. Willie looked up and said, "Well, good morning to you, Lucy Begay. What brings you out in this cold weather?"

"I have a necklace to sell," Mrs. Begay said. "It belonged to my aunt from Chinle." She opened the case and showed Willie a beautiful squash blossom necklace.

"That's a beaut! Old, too. Looks like from the thirties."

"I think that's about right," Mrs. Begay said quietly.

Ofelia came over to the case and looked over Mrs. Begay's shoulder. As she got closer, she noticed the woman's hair. She gasped! It was exactly like Doña Clementina's. Mrs. Begay looked back in surprise. Ofelia recovered by pretending to choke. "Excuse me! I'm sorry. It is so dry today!" She coughed repeatedly to dissimulate.

Mrs. Begay handed Willie her necklace and left the shop quietly. As she was leaving, Ofelia looked at Willie with expectant eyes. She waited until the woman closed the door behind her and then said, "Did you see her hair?"

"Don't even think about it!" Willie said. "Unlike you, I would never ask an Indian woman to part with her hair."

"Oh no! I don't want her hair!" Ofelia exclaimed. "I just wanted you to see it. Doña Clementina's hair was just like hers! Could you replicate that color and thickness of hair?"

"Missy, when it comes to hair, I can replicate anything. You remember Rock Hudson in *Winchester 73*?"

"No, I can't say that I do. I'm not much of a western film buff," Ofelia said.

"Well, he plays an Indian in that movie, and yours truly made the wig! You wanna braid like Lucy Begay's, that's what you'll get!"

"How soon can you get it done?" Ofelia asked.

"Oh, I would say by Saturday, at the latest."

"Mr. Reason, I don't have until Saturday."

"These things take time."

Ofelia looked disappointed.

"I think I have everything I need but . . . how about in two days? Come by two days from today, and I'll have the braid ready for you."

Ofelia thanked him profusely. Willie and Mr. Martinez shook hands, and Ofelia and Mr. Martinez went next door to the Double LL to have some coffee.

When they sat down in the brown vinyl booth, Ofelia reached over and patted Mr. Martinez's hand. "Thank you so much for your help!"

"Don't mention it. You want to have some breakfast?"

All of a sudden Ofelia was starving. The cramps from the dysentery had gone away, and she was ready to wolf down two eggs over easy with ham and hash browns.

As she ate her breakfast, she and Mr. Martinez talked.

"I guess we'd better have our breakfast and get back on the road in case it starts snowing again," Ofelia said, sprinkling pepper on her eggs.

"I think you should lie low for the next two days, Miss Ofelia, until you can get that braid in this guy's hands." Mr. Martinez suggested that she bunk at the Double LL until the braid was ready.

"I have no clothes, nothing. I can't stay here without going back and getting some things."

"My advice to you is to get down to Kmart and get yourself some bare necessities, then just sit tight and watch the tube for two days."

Mr. Martinez drove Ofelia down to Kmart, and she bought some flannel pajamas, socks, cotton underwear, toothbrush, and toothpaste. By the time he drove her back to the Double LL, the sun was starting to set. They said their good-byes, and Mr. Martinez promised to come back for her in two days.

Ofelia passed the time watching daytime television, reading old *McCall's* and *Reader's Digest* magazines from the motel lobby, and walking around the metropolis of Winslow.

Two days later she got up early and went into El Porvenir to pick up the braid. Willie had it all wrapped up in dark blue tissue paper.

Ofelia opened up the parcel. "This is it!" she exclaimed.

Willie looked pleased with himself.

"Thank you so much, Mr. Reason." She thanked Willie a few more times before she returned to check out of the motel. Just then Mr. Martinez was driving into the parking lot. While she paid, he went to say good-bye to Willie.

They got into Mr. Martinez's truck and drove out of Winslow. Mr. Martinez turned to Ofelia and said, "Your friend Rogelio has been coming to your house two or three times a day. I wouldn't be surprised if he's there now, waiting for you."

"Well, I can't wait to give him what he wants so I can get on with my life," Ofelia said, looking out at the dark blue hills topped with snow. Mr. Martinez turned the radio on low to a country western station, and they drove in peace all the way to Flagstaff. The snow had begun to melt, but that is when it is the coldest. Mr. Martinez drove Ofelia right to her door. She got out quickly and took out the keys. She was struggling with the sticky key when she heard the phone ringing urgently. She burst through the door and ran in and picked up the phone. "Hello? Hello?" The line was dead.

Mr. Martinez was standing in the doorway. Ofelia turned to him and said, "Do you want to come in for a few minutes? I can make us some coffee."

"No, I'd better go bring some wood in. It's going to be pretty cold tonight."

Ofelia went up to him and hugged him. "Thank you so much! You have been very kind to me."

"I'll keep my eyes peeled for our friend Rogelio," Mr. Martinez said as he left Ofelia's apartment.

Ofelia found the mercado bag with the chocolate and the chiles that Doña Cleme had sent Rogelio. She found the piece of red velvet, took the braid out of her bag, and wrapped it in the velvet cloth. She put everything back into the mercado bag and left it on the kitchen table.

The coffee hadn't finished brewing when she heard pounding on the door. Ofelia could see through the silhouette of the blind that it was Rogelio. She lifted the blind to give him some time to see that she was going to open the door. She thought that perhaps he would calm down once he saw her, but he didn't. He just seemed to get more enraged. Taking a closer look at the young man, she could see that he was as purple as an eggplant; his black hair was standing on end, and he had a wild look in his eyes. Ofelia took a deep breath and slowly opened the door. Before she had a chance to ask him in, the young man bolted into the apartment.

"Come in," Ofelia said. A cold blast of air came in with him. She went to close the door when she noticed Mr. Martinez had stepped in the threshold.

"Can I come in too? It's pretty cold out here."

Ofelia smiled gratefully and said, "I believe the two of you have met."

Rogelio paced back and forth in a small area of the living room, and Ofelia was afraid of what he would do next. Mr. Martinez stood aside quietly, but his presence made Ofelia feel safe.

Then in the sweetest voice she could conjure up, she said, "Rogelio, please sit down. Would you like some coffee?"

Rogelio lunged at Ofelia and said, "You have my mother's hair! She cut it off and gave it to you and I want it back!"

"Look, Rogelio, let me tell you what happened. When I went to see your mother, she was so upset that …" Rogelio was beyond listening to an explanation.

"I don't want to hear it! You know what I want!"

"Yes, of course I do," she said as she handed him the mercado bag.

Rogelio took the bag and rummaged through it and found the braid. He held it in his hands, and tears welled up in his eyes.

"I'm sorry if I caused you anguish. I meant no harm," Ofelia said.

"I didn't come here for explanations. I'm getting the hell out of this godforsaken place. Since the day that I met you, my life has been nothing but misery!"

Rogelio grabbed the mercado bag, tucked the braid under his arm, and stormed out the door as Mr. Martinez held it open for him.

A white van was waiting for him out in the street. Several cardboard boxes and suitcases were tied to the top of it. Ofelia felt relief to know that Rogelio was on his way out of town and out of her life forever.

Just then the phone rang again. Ofelia picked it up and wearily said, "Hello?"

"Hola, Ofelia, ¿Cómo está? Soy Lupita."

Ofelia's heart felt like it was in her throat. "Lupita? Is everything all right?"

"Well, I called to tell you," she was shouting through the phone. There was a lot of static on the line. "Hello? Are you there?"

"Yes! I'm here! Speak up, Lupita. What is it?"

"I called to tell you that on my way to Ocotlán from Oaxaca a few days ago, I took the bus to Doña Cleme's house."

"Yes? Is she all right?" Ofelia was waiting to hear the bad news. "What is it?"

"Well, I took the bus and I was talking to the driver and he remembers you. He remembers taking you to Doña Cleme's! And you'll never imagine what happened. Doña Cleme's better. She all but recovered!"

"Thank God!" Ofelia sighed in relief.

Lupita continued amidst the static of the bad connection. "But Ofelia, the most interesting part is that Antonio, the bus driver, found Doña Cleme's braid! It was under the seat. You must have dropped it when you got on the bus."

"Oh my God!" Ofelia said as she felt the blood drain out of her head. She sat down on the bed; she couldn't believe it.

"Lupita, listen, there has been a terrible mistake. Listen to me! I need to tell you ..."

"Don't worry, Ofelia, everything is all right. When Rogelio finds out that we found the braid, he won't be mad anymore."

"No, you don't understand." The static got really bad, and Ofelia couldn't hear a thing Lupita was saying.

"Can I call you back?" Ofelia said frantically.

"No, I'm at the telefónica."

"Give me a number where I can reach you. I have to explain something to you, and I'm afraid we are going to get cut off!"

"Don't worry! I just wanted to let you know what happened.

Oh, and by the way, Doña Cleme says hello. She said you were a nice lady."

Ofelia yelled into the phone, "Listen, Lupita! You have to listen!" Ofelia burst out with her story and told Lupita the truth. "And when I realized that I had lost the braid and that Rogelio would come after me, I had a braid made, just like Doña Cleme's, and well" — Ofelia hesitated, wondering if Lupita was taking in the bizarre account of what had happened — "I gave it to Rogelio and he's gone. He left town; I just gave the braid to him and now he's gone! He thinks he's got his mother's braid!" Ofelia was agitated, discouraged, and scared. As she was retelling the story, she realized how genuinely strange the whole thing was and then felt foolish and humiliated about the entire episode. The line was silent, and Ofelia thought she had lost the connection. "Hello? Lupita, are you there? Hello?" Ofelia yelled into the phone.

The girl quietly replied, "I don't know what to say, Ofelia."

Ofelia felt faint. She sighed deeply. "Lupita, I know it sounds crazy, but I didn't know what else to do."

"Let me call you back," Lupita said, and she hung up.

Mr. Martinez had been standing in the living room all this time. Ofelia came out, white as a sheet.

"Well, it seems that I am still not done with Rogelio," Ofelia said as she sat on the couch in shock.

Mr. Martinez had a gray pallor; his lips were shut tight; he looked out the window.

Ofelia went to pour the coffee when the phone rang again. It was Lupita. "Ofelia, Doña Clementina wants to talk to you."

"Oh, great!" Ofelia whispered to herself as the old lady picked up the phone.

She could hear Doña Clementina's soft, thin voice. "Ofelia, hija, how are you?"

"I'm fine, Doña Clementina, but as you now know, I'm in quite a predicament."

"I'm so glad you found the braid, dear."

Ofelia was confused. "I found the braid?"

"Yes, Lupita told me all about it. You lost my braid but then you found it and gave it to my son. I hope he wasn't rude to you. He has a very bad temper, bless his heart."

Ofelia knew she should explain but had no energy to retell the story. "But Doña Clementina, you don't understand."

"I understand perfectly. You lost the braid but then you found it and you gave it to my son. He feels better, I feel better, and you should feel better too. It's out of your hands now. You did me a great favor. Thank you."

"But didn't Lupita tell you?" Ofelia stammered.

There was a long pause, and then Doña Clementina said, "Yes, she explained everything to me. Don't worry, hija, it's all been taken care of."

"I'm not sure if I've been clear. Let me explain ..." Ofelia said, taking a deep breath and getting ready to go through the whole account again.

"The braid has been found and it is in the hands of my son and that is all that we care about. We understand each other perfectly, hija. Don't give it another thought." Then Doña Clementina changed the subject and said, "And when are you coming back to see me, hija?"

"To see you?" Suddenly everything was obvious to Ofelia. "Oh, Doña Clementina, you are too kind!"

"It is you who are kind, my dear."

"Thank you! Thank you so much, Doña Clementina."

"Que dios te bendiga, hija," the old woman said and hung up.

Stunned, Ofelia put down the receiver and walked into the

living room to talk to Mr. Martinez, but he had left. She appreciated his respect for her privacy; he was astute enough to know that she needed to be alone to let the reality of the last few days sink in. Her bedroom was in disarray, and she started putting her clothes away. After she had put the room back in order, she went in to take a hot shower. Ofelia let the hot water stream down over her neck and shoulders; she could feel the tension leaving her body. She wrapped herself in a thick terry-cloth robe, went to the phone, and called Mr. Martinez.

"Martinez here," he answered.

"It's me."

Mr. Martinez was concerned. "Are you all right?"

"Do you want to hear the last part of the story?"

"Only if it's a happy ending."

"What do you say if we go down to the Mormon Lake Lodge and get ourselves a couple of steaks I'll tell you all about it? My treat."

"I don't know, young lady. I'm an old man. I can't live on the edge like you do," Mr. Martinez said with laughter in his voice.

"I promise this is about as exciting as it gets. I'm really a very ordinary, even boring person."

"You driving? I'm gonna need to have a couple of beers to unwind."

"I'm driving," Ofelia said. She smiled to herself as she hung up. Ofelia had a feeling she and Mr. Martinez would be good friends for a long time. She always managed to meet interesting people.

About the Author

ANA CONSUELO MATIELLA was born in Nogales, Sonora, Mexico, and raised in the border towns of Ambos Nogales by a clan of Mexicans and Spaniards. She graduated from Nogales High School in 1970 and attended Northern Arizona University for her undergraduate work, receiving a B.S. in sociology in 1976. She received her M.A. in English as a Second Language from the University of Arizona in 1982.

Ms. Matiella is the author and editor of several books on multicultural education and produces fotonovelas on various educational topics. She is a columnist for the *Santa Fe New Mexican,* and her work has been anthologized in *Walking the Twilight: Women Writers of the Southwest* (Northland Publishing 1994). She is at work on a novel.